The Mummy's Foot
AND OTHER STORIES

The Mummy's Foot

AND OTHER STORIES

THEOPHILE GAUTIER

ÆGYPAN PRESS

The Mummy's Foot and Other Stories
A publication of
ÆGYPAN PRESS
www.aegypan.com

Table of Contents

The Mummy's Foot

I had entered, in an idle mood, the shop of one of those curiosity-venders, who are called marchands de bric-à-brac in that Parisian argot which is so perfectly unintelligible elsewhere in France.

You have doubtless glanced occasionally through the windows of some of these shops, which have become so numerous now that it is fashionable to buy antiquated furniture, and that every petty stock-broker thinks he must have his chambre au moyen age.

There is one thing there which clings alike to the shop of the dealer in old iron, the wareroom of the tapestry-maker, the laboratory of the chemist, and the studio of the painter: – in all those gloomy dens where a furtive daylight filters in through the window-shutters, the most manifestly ancient thing is dust; – the cobwebs are more authentic than the guimp laces; and the old pear tree furniture on exhibition is actually younger than the mahogany which arrived but yesterday from America.

The warehouse of my bric-à-brac dealer was a veritable Capharnaum; all ages and all nations seemed to have made their rendezvous there; an Etruscan lamp of red clay stood upon a Boule cabinet, with ebony panels, brightly striped by lines of inlaid brass; a duchess of the court of Louis XV nonchalantly extended her fawnlike feet under a massive table of the time of Louis XIII with heavy spiral supports of oak, and carven designs of chimeras and foliage intermingled.

Upon the denticulated shelves of several sideboards glittered immense Japanese dishes with red and blue designs relieved by gilded hatching; side by side with enameled works by Bernard Palissy, representing serpents, frogs, and lizards in relief.

From disemboweled cabinets escaped cascades of silver-lustrous Chinese silks and waves of tinsel, which an oblique sunbeam shot through with luminous beads; while portraits of every era, in frames more or less tarnished, smiled through their yellow varnish.

The striped breastplate of a damascened suit of Milanese armor glittered in one corner; Loves and Nymphs of porcelain; Chinese Grotesques, vases of celadon and crackleware; Saxon and old Souvres cups encumbered the shelves and nooks of the apartment.

The dealer followed me closely through the tortuous way contrived between the piles of furniture; warding off with his hands the hazardous sweep of my coat-skirts; watching my elbows with the uneasy attention of an antiquarian and a usurer.

It was a singular face that of the merchant: – an immense skull, polished like a knee, and surrounded by a thin aureole of white hair, which brought out the clear salmon tint of his complexion all the more strikingly, lent him a false aspect of patriarchal bonhomie, counteracted, however, by the scintillation of two little yellow eyes which trembled in their orbits like two louis-d'or upon quicksilver. The curve of his nose presented an aquiline silhouette, which suggested the Oriental or Jewish type. His hands – thin, slender, full of nerves which projected like strings upon the finger-board of a violin, and armed with claws like those on the terminations of bats' wings – shook with senile trembling; but those convulsively agitated hands became firmer than steel pincers or lobsters' claws when they lifted any precious article – an onyx cup, a Venetian glass, or a dish of Bohemian crystal. This strange old man had an aspect so thoroughly rabbinical and cabalistic that he would have been burned on the mere testimony of his face three centuries ago.

"Will you not buy something from me today, sir? Here is a Malay kreese with a blade undulating like flame: look at those grooves contrived for the blood to run along, those teeth set backwards so as to tear out the entrails in withdrawing the weapon – it is a fine character of ferocious arm, and will look well in your collection: this two-handed sword is very beautiful – it is the work of Josepe de la Hera; and this colichemarde, with its fenestrated guard – what a superb specimen of handicraft!"

"No; I have quite enough weapons and instruments of carnage; – I want a small figure, something which will suit me as a paper-weight; for I cannot endure those trumpery bronzes which the stationers sell, and which may be found on everybody's desk."

The old gnome foraged among his ancient wares, and finally arranged before me some antique bronzes – so-called, at least; fragments of malachite; little Hindu or Chinese idols – a kind of poussah toys in jadestone, representing the incarnations of Brahma or Vishnu, and wonderfully appropriate to the very undivine office of holding papers and letters in place.

I was hesitating between a porcelain dragon, all constellated with warts – its mouth formidable with bristling tusks and ranges of teeth – and an abominable little Mexican fetish, representing the god Zitziliputzili au naturel, when I caught sight of a charming foot, which I at first took for a fragment of some antique Venus.

It had those beautiful ruddy and tawny tints that lend to Florentine bronze that warm living look so much preferable to the grey-green aspect of common bronzes, which might easily be mistaken for statues in a state of putrefaction: satiny gleams played over its rounded forms, doubtless polished by the amorous kisses of twenty centuries; for it seemed a Corinthian bronze, a work of the best era of art – perhaps molded by Lysippus himself.

"That foot will be my choice," I said to the merchant, who regarded me with an ironical and saturnine air, and held out the object desired that I might examine it more fully.

I was surprised at its lightness; it was not a foot of metal, but in sooth a foot of flesh – an embalmed foot – a mummy's foot: on examining it still more closely the very grain of the skin, and the almost imperceptible lines impressed upon it by the texture of the bandages, became perceptible. The toes were slender and delicate, and terminated by perfectly formed nails, pure and transparent as agates; the great toe, slightly separated from the rest, afforded a happy contrast, in the antique style, to the position of the other toes, and lent it an aërial lightness – the grace of a bird's foot; – the sole, scarcely streaked by a few almost imperceptible cross lines, afforded evidence that it had never touched the bare ground, and had only come in contact with the finest matting of Nile rushes, and the softest carpets of panther skin.

"Ha, ha! – you want the foot of the Princess Hermonthis," – exclaimed the merchant, with a strange giggle, fixing his owlish eyes upon me – "ha, ha, ha! – for a paper-weight! – an original idea! – artistic idea! Old Pharaoh would certainly have been surprised had someone told him that the foot of his adored daughter would be used for a paper-weight after he had had a mountain of granite hollowed out as a receptacle for the triple coffin, painted and gilded – covered with hieroglyphics and beautiful paintings of the Judgment of Souls," – continued the queer little merchant, half audibly, as though talking to himself!

"How much will you charge me for this mummy fragment?"

"Ah, the highest price I can get; for it is a superb piece: if I had the match of it you could not have it for less than five hundred francs; – the daughter of a Pharaoh! nothing is more rare."

"Assuredly that is not a common article; but, still, how much do you want? In the first place let me warn you that all my wealth consists of just five louis: I can buy anything that costs five louis, but nothing dearer; – you might search my vest pockets and most secret drawers without even finding one poor – five-franc piece more."

"Five louis for the foot of the Princess Hermonthis! that is very little, very little indeed; 'tis an authentic foot," muttered the merchant, shaking his head, and imparting a peculiar rotary motion to his eyes.

"Well, take it, and I will give you the bandages into the bargain," he added, wrapping the foot in an ancient damask rag – "very fine! real damask – Indian damask which has never been redyed; it is strong, and yet it is soft," he mumbled, stroking the frayed tissue with his fingers, through the trade-acquired habit which moved him to praise even an object of so little value that he himself deemed it only worth the giving away.

He poured the gold coins into a sort of mediaeval alms-purse hanging at his belt, repeating:

"The foot of the Princess Hermonthis, to be used for a paper-weight!"

Then turning his phosphorescent eyes upon me, he exclaimed in a voice strident as the crying of a cat which has swallowed a fish-bone:

"Old Pharaoh will not be well pleased; he loved his daughter – the dear man!"

"You speak as if you were a contemporary of his: you are old enough, goodness knows! but you do not date back to the Pyramids of Egypt," I answered, laughingly, from the threshold. I went home, delighted with my acquisition.

With the idea of putting it to profitable use as soon as possible, I placed the foot of the divine Princess Hermonthis upon a heap of papers scribbled over with verses, in themselves an undecipherable mosaic work of erasures; articles freshly begun; letters forgotten, and posted in the table drawer instead of the letterbox – an error to which absent-minded people are peculiarly liable. The effect was charming, bizarre, and romantic.

Well satisfied with this embellishment, I went out with the gravity and price becoming one who feels that he has the ineffable advantage over all the passers-by whom he elbows, of possessing a piece of the Princess Hermonthis, daughter of Pharaoh.

I looked upon all who did not possess, like myself, a paper-weight so authentically Egyptian, as very ridiculous people; and it seemed to me that the proper occupation of every sensible man should consist in the mere fact of having a mummy's foot upon his desk.

Happily I met some friends, whose presence distracted me in my infatuation with this new acquisition: I went to dinner with them; for I could not very well have dined with myself.

When I came back that evening, with my brain slightly confused by a few glasses of wine, a vague whiff of Oriental perfume delicately titillated my olfactory nerves: the heat of the room had warmed the natron, bitumen, and myrrh in which the paraschistes, who cut open the bodies of the dead, had bathed the corpse of the princess; – it was a perfume at once sweet and penetrating – a perfume that four thousand years had not been able to dissipate.

The Dream of Egypt was Eternity: her odors have the solidity of granite, and endure as long.

I soon drank deeply from the black cup of sleep: for a few hours all remained opaque to me; Oblivion and Nothingness inundated me with their somber waves.

Yet light gradually dawned upon the darkness of my mind; dreams commenced to touch me softly in their silent flight.

The eyes of my soul were opened; and I beheld my chamber as it actually was; I might have believed myself awake, but for a vague consciousness which assured me that I slept, and that something fantastic was about to take place.

The odor of the myrrh had augmented in intensity; and I felt a slight headache, which I very naturally attributed to several glasses of champagne that we had drunk to the unknown gods and our future fortunes.

I peered through my room with a feeling of expectation which I saw nothing to justify: every article of furniture was in its proper place; the lamp, softly shaded by its globe of ground crystal, burned upon its bracket; the watercolor sketches shone under their Bohemian glass; the curtains hung down languidly; everything wore an aspect of tranquil slumber.

After a few moments, however, all this calm interior appeared to become disturbed; the woodwork cracked stealthily; the ash-covered log suddenly emitted a jet of blue flame; and the disks of the pateras seemed like great metallic eyes, watching, like myself, for the things which were about to happen.

My eyes accidentally fell upon the desk where I had placed the foot of the Princess Hermonthis.

Instead of remaining quiet – as behooved a foot which had been embalmed for four thousand years – it commenced to act in a nervous manner; contracted itself, and leaped over the papers like a startled frog; – one would have imagined that it had suddenly been brought into contact with a galvanic battery: I could distinctly hear the dry sound made by its little heel, hard as the hoof of a gazelle.

I became rather discontented with my acquisition, inasmuch as I wished my paper-weights to be of a sedentary disposition, and thought it very unnatural that feet should walk about without legs; and I commenced to experience a feeling closely akin to fear.

Suddenly I saw the folds of my bed-curtain stir; and heard a bumping sound, like that caused by some person hopping on one foot across the floor. I must confess I became alternately hot and cold; that I felt a strange wind chill my back; and that my suddenly rising hair caused my nightcap to execute a leap of several yards.

The bed-curtains opened and I beheld the strangest figure imaginable before me.

It was a young girl of a very deep coffee-brown complexion, like the bayadere Amani, and possessing the purest Egyptian type of perfect beauty: her eyes were almond-shaped and oblique, with eyebrows so black that they seemed blue; her nose was exquisitely chiseled, almost Greek in its delicacy of outline; and she might indeed have been taken for a Corinthian statue of bronze, but for the prominence of her cheekbones and the slightly African fullness of her lips, which compelled one to recognize her as belonging beyond all doubt to the hieroglyphic race which dwelt upon the banks of the Nile.

Her arms, slender and spindle-shaped, like those of very young girls, were encircled by a peculiar kind of metal bands and bracelets of glass beads; her hair was all twisted into little cords; and she wore upon her bosom a little idol-figure of green paste, bearing a whip with seven lashes, which proved it to be an image of Isis: her brow was adorned with a shining plate of gold; and a few traces of paint relieved the coppery tint of her cheeks.

As for her costume, it was very odd indeed. Fancy a pagne or skirt all formed of little strips of material bedizened with red and black hieroglyphics, stiffened with bitumen, and apparently belonging to a freshly unbandaged mummy.

In one of those sudden flights of thought so common in dreams I heard the hoarse falsetto of the bric-à-brac dealer, repeating like a monotonous refrain the phrase he had uttered in his shop with so enigmatical an intonation:

"Old Pharaoh will not be well pleased: he loved his daughter, the dear man!"

One strange circumstance, which was not at all calculated to restore my equanimity, was that the apparition had but one foot; the other was broken off at the ankle!

She approached the table where the foot was starting and fidgeting about more than ever, and there supported herself upon the edge of the desk. I saw her eyes fill with pearly-gleaming tears.

Although she had not as yet spoken, I fully comprehended the thoughts which agitated her: she looked at her foot – it was indeed her own – with an exquisitely graceful expression of coquettish sadness; but the foot leaped and ran hither and thither, as though impelled on steel springs.

Twice or thrice she extended her hand to seize it, but could not succeed.

Then commenced between the Princess Hermonthis and her foot – which appeared to be endowed with a special life of its own – a very fantastic dialogue in a most ancient Coptic tongue, such as might have been spoken thirty centuries ago in the syrinxes of the land of Ser: luckily, I understood Coptic perfectly well that night.

The Princess Hermonthis cried, in a voice sweet and vibrant as the tones of a crystal bell:

"Well, my dear little foot, you always flee from me; yet I always took good care of you. I bathed you with perfumed water in a bowl of alabaster; I smoothed your heel with pumice-stone mixed with palm oil; your nails were cut with golden scissors and polished with a hippopotamus tooth; I was careful to select tatbebs for you, painted and embroidered and turned up at the toes, which were the envy of all the young girls in Egypt: you wore on your great toe rings bearing the device of the sacred Scarabaeus; and you supported one of the lightest bodies that a lazy foot could sustain."

The foot replied, in a pouting and chagrined tone:

"You know well that I do not belong to myself any longer; – I have been bought and paid for; the old merchant knew what he was about; he bore you a grudge for having refused to espouse him; – this is an ill turn which he has done you. The Arab who violated your royal coffin in the subterranean pit of the necropolis of Thebes was sent thither by him: he desired to prevent you from being present at the reunion of the shadowy nations in the cities below. Have you five pieces of gold for my ransom?"

"Alas, no! – my jewels, my rings, my purses of gold and silver, they were all stolen from me," answered the Princess Hermonthis, with a sob.

"Princess," I then exclaimed, "I never retained anybody's foot unjustly; – even though you have not got the five louis which it cost me, I present it to you gladly: I should feel unutterably wretched to think that I were the cause of so amiable a person as the Princess Hermonthis being lame."

I delivered this discourse in a royally gallant, troubadour tone, which must have astonished the beautiful Egyptian girl.

She turned a look of deepest gratitude upon me; and her eyes shone with bluish gleams of light.

She took her foot – which surrendered itself willingly this time – like a woman about to put on her little shoe, and adjusted it to her leg with much skill.

This operation over, she took a few steps about the room, as though to assure herself that she was really no longer lame.

"Ah, how pleased my father will be! – he who was so unhappy because of my mutilation, and who from the moment of my birth set a whole nation at work to hollow me out a tomb so deep that he might preserve me intact until that last day, when souls must be weighed in the balance of Amenthi! Come with me to my father; – he will receive you kindly; for you have given me back my foot."

I thought this proposition natural enough. I arrayed myself in a dressing gown of large-flowered pattern, which lent me a very Pharaonic aspect; hurriedly put on a pair of Turkish slippers, and informed the Princess Hermonthis that I was ready to follow her.

Before starting, Hermonthis took from her neck the little idol of green paste, and laid it on the scattered sheets of paper which covered the table.

"It is only fair," she observed smilingly, "that I should replace your paper-weight."

She gave me her hand, which felt soft and cold, like the skin of a serpent; and we departed.

We passed for some time with the velocity of an arrow through a fluid and greyish expanse, in which half-formed silhouettes flitted swiftly by us, to right and left.

For an instant we saw only sky and sea.

A few moments later obelisks commenced to tower in the distance: pylons and vast flights of steps guarded by sphinxes became clearly outlined against the horizon.

We had reached our destination. The princess conducted me to the mountain of rose-colored granite, in the face of which appeared an opening so narrow and low that it would have been difficult to distinguish it from the fissures in the rock, had not its location been marked by two stelae wrought with sculptures.

Hermonthis kindled a torch, and led the way before me.

We traversed corridors hewn through the living rock: their walls, covered with hieroglyphics and paintings of allegorical processions, might well have occupied thousands of arms for thousands of years in their formation; – these corridors, of interminable length, opened into square chambers, in the midst of which pits had been contrived, through which we descended by cramp-irons or spiral stairways; – these pits again conducted us into other chambers, opening into other corridors, likewise decorated with painted sparrow-hawks, serpents coiled in circles, the symbols of the tau and pedum – prodigious works of art which no living eye can ever examine – interminable legends of granite which only the dead have time to read through all eternity.

At last we found ourselves in a hall so vast, so enormous, so immeasurable, that the eye could not reach its limits; files of monstrous columns stretched far out of sight on every side, between which twinkled livid stars of yellowish flame; – points of light which revealed further depths incalculable in the darkness beyond.

The Princess Hermonthis still held my hand, and graciously saluted the mummies of her acquaintance.

My eyes became accustomed to the dim twilight, and objects became discernible.

I beheld the kings of the subterranean races seated upon thrones – grand old men, though dry, withered, wrinkled like parchment, and blackened with naphtha and bitumen – all wearing pshents of gold, and breastplaces and gorgets glittering with precious stones; their eyes immovably fixed like the eyes of sphinxes, and their long beards whitened by the snow of centuries. Behind them stood their peoples, in the stiff and constrained posture enjoined by Egyptian art, all eternally preserving the attitude prescribed by the hieratic code. Behind these nations, the cats, ibises, and crocodiles contemporary with them – rendered monstrous of aspect by their swathing bands – mewed, flapped their wings, or extended their jaws in a saurian giggle.

All the Pharaohs were there – Cheops, Chephrenes, Psammetichus, Sesostris, Amenotaph – all the dark rulers of the pyramids and syrinxes – on yet higher thrones sat Chronos and Xixouthros – who was contemporary with the deluge; and Tubal Cain, who reigned before it.

The beard of King Xixouthros had grown seven times around the granite table, upon which he leaned, lost in deep reverie – and buried in dreams.

Further back, through a dusty cloud, I beheld dimly the seventy-two pre-Adamite Kings, with their seventy-two peoples – forever passed away.

After permitting me to gaze upon this bewildering spectacle a few moments, the Princess Hermonthis presented me to her father Pharaoh, who favored me with a most gracious nod.

"I have found my foot again! – I have found my foot!" cried the Princess, clapping her little hands together with every sign of frantic joy: "it was this gentleman who restored it to me."

The races of Kemi, the races of Nahasi – all the black, bronzed, and copper-colored nations repeated in chorus:

"The Princess Hermonthis has found her foot again!"

Even Xixouthros himself was visibly affected.

He raised his heavy eyelids, stroked his mustache with his fingers, and turned upon me a glance weighty with centuries.

"By Oms, the dog of Hell, and Tmei, daughter of the Sun and of Truth! this is a brave and worthy lad!" exclaimed Pharaoh, pointing to me with his scepter, which was terminated with a lotus-flower.

"What recompense do you desire?"

Filled with that daring inspired by dreams in which nothing seems impossible, I asked him for the hand of the Princess Hermonthis; – the hand seemed to me a very proper antithetic recompense for the foot.

Pharaoh opened wide his great eyes of glass in astonishment at my witty request.

"What country do you come from? and what is your age?"

"I am a Frenchman; and I am twenty-seven years old, venerable Pharaoh."

"– Twenty-seven years old! and he wishes to espouse the Princess Hermonthis, who is thirty centuries old!" cried out at once all the Thrones and all the Circles of Nations.

Only Hermonthis herself did not seem to think my request unreasonable.

"If you were even only two thousand years old," replied the ancient King, "I would willingly give you the Princess; but the disproportion is too great; and, besides, we must give our daughters husbands who will last well: you do not know how to preserve yourselves any longer; even those who died only fifteen centuries ago are already no more than a handful of dust; – behold! my flesh is solid as basalt; my bones are bars of steel!

"I shall be present on the last day of the world, with the same body and the same features which I had during my lifetime: my daughter Hermonthis will last longer than a statue of bronze.

"Then the last particles of your dust will have been scattered abroad by the winds; and even Isis herself, who was able to find the atoms of Osiris, would scarce be able to recompose your being.

"See how vigorous I yet remain, and how mighty is my grasp," he added, shaking my hand in the English fashion with a strength that buried my rings in the flesh of my fingers.

He squeezed me so hard that I awoke, and found my friend Alfred shaking me by the arm to make me get up.

"O you everlasting sleeper! – must I have you carried out into the middle of the street, and fireworks exploded in your ears? It is after noon; don't you recollect your promise to take me with you to see M. Aguado's Spanish pictures?"

"God! I forgot all, all about it," I answered, dressing myself hurriedly; "we will go there at once; I have the permit lying on my desk."

I started to find it; – but fancy my astonishment when I beheld, instead of the mummy's foot I had purchased the evening before, the little green paste idol left in its place by the Princess Hermonthis!

One of Cleopatra's Nights

I

About eighteen hundred years ago from the moment we write these lines, a cange magnificently gilded and painted came down the Nile with all the rapidity which can be got from fifty long flat oars crawling on the scratched water like the feet of a gigantic scarabeus beetle.

This cange was narrow, elongated in shape, tilted at the two ends in the form of a crescent moon, slim in its proportions, and marvelously fashioned for speed; a ram's head surmounted by a golden ball armed the point of the prow, and showed that the craft belonged to a personage of royal rank.

In the center of the boat was erected a cabin with a flat roof, a kind of naos, or tent of honor, colored and gilded, with a molding of palm leaves, and four little square windows.

Two rooms, covered in the same way with hieroglyphics, occupied the ends of the crescent; one of them, bigger than the other, had, juxtaposed, a story of less height, like the châteaux gaillards of those quaint galleys of the sixteenth century drawn by Della Bella; the smaller, which served as quarters for the pilot, ended in a triangular poop-rail.

The rudder was made of two immense oars, set on many-colored posts, and trailing in the water behind the bark like the webbed feet of a swan; heads adorned with the pschent and wearing on the chin the allegorical horn, were sculptured by handfuls along those great oars which the pilot maneuvered standing erect on the roof of the cabin.

He was a sunburned man, fawn-colored like new bronze, with blue glistening high-lights, his eyes tilted at the corners, his hair very black and plaited into little strings, his mouth wide spread, his cheekbones prominent, his ears sitting out from his skull, the Egyptian type in all its purity. A narrow loin-cloth tied on his hips, and five or six twists of glass beads and amulets, composed all his costume.

He seemed to be the only inhabitant of the cange, for the rowers, bent over their oars, and hidden by the gunwale, only made their presence divined by the symmetrical movement of the oar-blades, opening like the spokes of a fan on each flank of the bark, and falling again into the stream after a slight moment of suspension.

No puff of air stirred the atmosphere, and the big triangular sail of the cange, rolled up and tied with a silken cord along the lowered mast, showed that all hope of the wind rising had been abandoned.

The midday sun discharged its leaden arrows; the ash-colored ooze on the river's banks gave out flamboyant reflections; a hard light, dazzling and dusty because of its intensity, streamed down in torrents of flame; the azure of the sky was white with heat like metal in the furnace; a blazing reddish haze rose like smoke on the burning horizon. Not a cloud showed on that sky as unvarying and mournful as eternity.

The water of the Nile, dull and lusterless, seemed to be sleeping in its course, and to spread out in sheets of molten pewter. No breath wrinkled its surface, nor swayed on their stalks the flower cups of the lotus, as rigid as if they had been sculptured; only at distant intervals the leap of a bechir or a fahaka inflating the under part of his body, barely mirrored in the water a silver scale, and the oars of the cange seemed to tear with difficulty the fuliginous scum of the stagnant stream. The banks were deserted; a deep and solemn gloom weighed on that land which was never aught else than a mighty tomb, a land whose living inhabitants seemed never to have had any other occupation but that of embalming the dead. A sterile gloom, dry as pumice stone, without melancholy, without reverie, having no pearl-grey cloud to gaze at on the horizon, no secret spring in which to bathe its dusty feet; the gloom of the sphinx wearied with perpetually watching the desert, the sphinx who can never quit the granite pedestal on which it has sharpened its claws for twenty centuries.

The silence was so profound that one would have said that the whole world had become mute, or that the air had lost its power of conducting sound. The sole noise to be heard was the whispering and muffled laughter of the crocodiles, swooning with heat, who wallowed in the reeds of the river; or else some ibis who, tired of standing erect, one foot folded back under its body, his head between his shoulders, quitted his immobile station, and, roughly lashing the blue air with his white wings, went to perch anew on an obelisk or a palm tree.

The cange shot like an arrow through the water of the river, leaving behind it a silvery furrow which soon closed up; and some bubbles of foam, coming to the surface to burst, were the sole witnesses of the passage of the bark that was already out of sight.

The steep banks of the river, salmon and ochre colored, opened to the view like strips of papyrus between the double azure of the sky and the water, so alike in tone that the slim tongue of land which separated them seemed a pathway flung over an immense lake, so that it would have been difficult to decide if the Nile reflected the sky or if the sky reflected the Nile.

The spectacle changed every moment: now it was gigantic propylea that came to mirror in the river their shelving walls, set with large flat panels of quaint figures; pylons with splayed capitals, flights of stairs bordered with crouching sphinxes, caps with fluted lappets on their heads, and crossing over their pointed breasts their black basalt paws; inordinate palaces of which the severe horizontal lines of the entablature jutted out against the horizon, where the emblematic sphere opened its mysterious wings like an eagle with inordinate wing-spread; temples with enormous columns, thick like towers, on which, on a background of dazzling white, processions of hieroglyphic figures stood out conspicuously; all the marvelous creations of an architecture of Titans; now it was countrysides of desolating sterility; hills formed by little fragments of stone that had come from excavations and buildings, crumbs of that gigantic debauch of granite which lasted more than thirty centuries; mountains denuded of foliage by the heat, slashed and barred by black lines like the scars of a forest fire; mounds hunchbacked and misformed, squatting like the criocephalus of the tombs, their misshapen forms showing up against the edge of the sky; greenish clay, reddish ochre, tufa rock of a floury white, and from time to time, some steep slope of old rose-colored marble in which gaped the black mouths of the quarries.

This sterility was tempered by nothing at all; no oasis of foliage refreshed the gaze; green seemed a color unknown in this land; only at long intervals a scrawny palm tree sprawled on the horizon like a vegetable crab; a thorny cochineal fig tree brandished its steely leaves like bronze gloves; a safflower, finding a little humidity in the shade of a stump of a column, set off with a point of red the general uniformity.

After this rapid glance at the general aspect of the country, let us come back to the cange with its fifty rowers, and without announcing ourselves, let us enter without ceremony into the naos of honor.

The interior was painted in white with green arabesques, with nets of vermilion and gold flowers of fantastic shapes; a reed mat of extreme fineness covered the floor; at the end of the room stood a small bed with griffin feet, with a back arranged like a sofa or modern settee, a stool with four steps to ascend into it, and, a luxury singular enough according to our ideas of comfort, a kind of half circle of cedar wood, mounted on a pedestal, designed to encircle the back of the neck and to sustain the head of the person in bed.

On this strange pillow rested a very charming head, the head of a woman adored and divine, one look from whom lost half a world. She was the most complete woman who had ever lived, a type of wonder to whom the poets can add nothing, and whom dreamers find forever at the end of their dreams: there is no need to name Cleopatra.

Beside her Charmion, her favorite slave, waved a large fan of ibis feathers. A young girl sprinkled with a shower of scented water the little reed blinds with which the windows of the naos were furnished, so that the air might only enter there impregnated with freshness and perfumes.

Near the couch, in a vase of ribbonlike alabaster, with a slender neck, slim and sinuous in outline, recalling vaguely the profile of them a heron, was a bouquet of lotus flowers in water, some of them a celestial blue, others a delicate rose like the fingertips of Isis, the great goddess.

Cleopatra, this day, by caprice or policy, was not dressed in Grecian fashion: she had just been present at a panegyry, and she was returning to her summer palace in the cange, wearing the Egyptian costume that she had been wearing at the festival.

Our lady readers will perhaps be curious to know how Queen Cleopatra was dressed in returning from the Mammisi of Hermonthis, where were worshipped the trinity of the God Mandou, the Goddess Ritho, and their son Harphre; that is a satisfaction we can give them.

Queen Cleopatra had for headdress a kind of very light gold helmet formed by the body and wings of the sacred sparrow-hawk; the wings, smoothed down fan-wise on each side of her head, covered her temples, and stretched almost to her neck, leaving free at a little opening an ear more rosy and more delicately folded than the shell whence sprang Venus whom the Egyptians name Hathor; the tail of the bird occupied the place where our ladies twist their rolls of hair; its body, covered with feathers imbricated and painted in different enamels, enveloped the top of her head, and its neck, gracefully bent towards the forehead, made up with the head a kind of horn sparkling with jewels; a symbolic crest in the shape of a tower completed this elegant, although bizarre headdress. Hair, black as that of a night without stars, escaped from this helmet and flowed in long tresses down her fair shoulders, but a collar or gorget, ornamented with several rows of serpentine, of azerodrach, and of chrysoberyl, left, alas! only the commencement of those shoulders in sight; a linen robe with diagonal ribs, a mistlike cloth, woven from air, ventus textilis as Petronius says, swayed in white vapor round a beautiful body whose lines it softly shaded. This robe had half sleeves, fitting on the shoulders but cut away towards the elbow like our sabot sleeves, and showing a wonderful arm and a perfect hand, the arm clasped by six circles of gold and the hand adorned by a ring representing a scarabeus. A belt, of which the knotted ends hung down behind, marked the waist of this floating and free tunic; a short cloak with fringes completed the attire, and if some barbaric words do not affright the ears of Paris, we will add that this robe was called schenti and the short cloak calasiris.

As a last detail, let us say that Queen Cleopatra wore light sandals, very slim, bent back at the point and attached to the ankle like the shoes a la poulaine of the chatelaines of the Middle Ages.

All the same Queen Cleopatra had not the satisfied air of a woman sure that she is perfectly lovely and perfectly attired; she turned and twisted on her little couch, and her rather brusque movements deranged each moment the folds of her gauze conopeum which Charmion readjusted with inexhaustible patience and without ceasing to wield her fan.

"It is stifling in this room," said Cleopatra, "even if Phtha, the God of Fire, had set up his forges here, it wouldn't be hotter; the air is like a furnace." And she passed over her lips the tip of her little tongue, then stretched out her hand like an invalid who feels about for an absent cup.

Charmion, ever attentive, clapped her hands: a black slave, clad in a straight gown pleated like the skirts of the Albanians, with a leopard skin thrown over his shoulder, entered with the rapidity of an apparition, holding balanced on his left hand a tray laden with cups and slices of water-melon, and in the right a long jug furnished with a spout like a teapot.

The slave filled one of the cups, pouring into it from a height with a marvelous dexterity, and put it before the queen. Cleopatra touched the beverage with her lips, put it down beside her, and turning towards Charmion, her beautiful black eyes unctuous and lustrous from the living sparkle of light in them:

"Oh, Charmion," she said, "I am bored."

II

Charmion, foreseeing a confidence, made a face of grievous assent, and came near her mistress.

"I am horribly bored," went on Cleopatra, letting her arms hang loose as one discouraged and defeated, "this Egypt destroys me and crushes me; this sky with its implacable blue is more somber than the deep night of Erebus; never a cloud! never a shadow, and forever this red, dripping sun which stares like the eye of a Cyclops! See, Charmion, I would give a pearl for a drop of rain! From the enflamed eyeball of this sky of bronze has never yet fallen a single tear on the desolation of the earth; it is a huge tombstone, a dome of a necropolis, a sky dead and dried up like the mummies it covers! it weighs on my shoulders like a too heavy coat! it irks me and distresses me; it seems to me as if I could not rise to my full height without bruising my forehead against it; and then, this country is really a fearful country; everything here is somber, enigmatical, incomprehensible! Imagination here produces nothing but monstrous chimeras and inordinate monuments; this sort of architecture and art terrifies me; these colossi whose limbs fixed in stone, condemn them to rest eternally seated with their hands on their knees, tire me with their stupid immobility; they obsess my eyes and my horizon. When, then, will the giant come who will take them by the hand and relieve them from their twenty-century-long sentry duty? Granite itself wears out at last! What master do they await to leave the mountain that serves them for a seat, and to rise in token of respect? Of what invisible herd are those mighty sphinxes, crouching like watch-dogs, the guardians, that they never close an eyelid and hold forever their claws at attention? What is the matter with them, then, that they fix so obstinately their eyes of stone on eternity and infinity? What strange secret do their tightly closed lips lock in their breasts? Right and left, on whatever side one turns, there are only monsters frightful to look on, dogs with men's heads, men with dogs' heads, chimeras begotten of hideous matings in the gloomy depths of the syrinx bushes, Anubises, Typhons, Osirises, sparrow-hawks with yellow eyes that seem to look through you with their inquisitive regards, and to see beyond you things that cannot be told: a family of horrible animals and gods with scaly wings, with hooked beaks, with tearing claws, always ready to seize you and devour you, if you pass the threshold of the temple, and if you raise the corner of the veil!

"On the walls, on the columns, on the roofs, on the floors, on the palaces and on the temples, in the corridors and in the deepest pits of the cemeteries, down to the entrails of the earth where the light does not reach, where the torches go out for lack of air, and everywhere and always, interminable hieroglyphics, sculptured and painted, recounting in unintelligible language things that are no longer known, and which belong no doubt to creations that have vanished; prodigious buried buildings where a whole people is worn out to write the epitaph of a king! Mystery and granite, that is Egypt; a fine country for a young woman and a young queen!

"Only menacing and funereal symbols are to be seen, the pedum, the tau, allegorical globes, entwined serpents, balances where souls are weighed, the unknown, death, nothingness! For the only vegetation, pillars striped with bizarre characters; for alleys of trees, avenues of granite obelisks; for earth, immense paving stones of granite, so huge that each mountain could furnish only a single flagstone; for sky, roofs of granite; a palpable eternity, a bitter and perpetual sarcasm of the fragility and brevity of life! stairways made for strides of Titan, which the human foot cannot step over and which must be ascended with ladders; columns that a hundred arms could not encircle, labyrinths where one could walk a year without finding the exit! the vertigo of enormity, the intoxication of the gigantic, the inordinate effort of pride which would carve at all costs its name on the surface of the world!

"And besides, Charmion, I tell you, I have a thought that terrifies me; in other countries of the earth they bury their dead, and their ashes are soon mingled with the ground. Here one might say that the living have no other occupation than that of preserving the dead; powerful balms snatch them from destruction; all of them keep their form and their appearance; the soul evaporates, the mortal body remains; under this people are twenty peoples; each city has its feet on twenty layers of tombs; each generation that goes leaves a population of mummies in a city of darkness; under the father, you find the grandfather and the great-grandfather in his painted and gilded box, such as they were in their lifetime; and were you to excavate forever you would forever find more of them!

"When I think of those multitudes, swathed in their bands, of those myriads of dried-up specters which fill the funeral pits and which have lain there for two thousand years, face to face, in their silence that nothing comes to trouble, not even the noise that the worm of the tomb makes in his crawling, and who will be found there untouched after another two thousand years, with their cats, their crocodiles, their ibises, all the things that lived at the same time as they did, spasms of terror seize me, and I feel shudders run up my skin. What do they say to each other, since they still have lips, and since their souls, if the fantasy seized them to return, would find their bodies in the state in which they left them?

"Egypt is truly a sinister kingdom and very little fitted for me who am fond of laughter and folly; everything here encloses a mummy; that is the heart and core of everything. After a thousand detours it is there you finish; the pyramids hide a sarcophagus. All that is nothingness and folly. Rip open the sky with gigantic triangles of stone, you will not add an inch to your corpse! How can one rejoice and live in such a land where one breathes as perfume only the bitter odor of naphtha, and the bitumen that boils in the embalmers' kettles, where the floor of your room sounds hollow because the corridors of the hypogeum and the funeral pits stretch even under your dressing-room? To be the queen of the mummies; to have as gossips those statues in their stiff, constrained poses, that's a lot of fun! And yet, if to lighten the gloom, I had some passion in my heart, an interest in life, if I were in love with somebody or something, if I were loved! But I am not.

"That is why I am bored, Charmion; with love this sterile, surly Egypt would seem to me more charming than Greece with its ivory gods, its temples of white marble, its oleander woods, and its fountains of spring water. I would not think of the grotesque countenance of Anubis, nor of the terrors of the underground cities."

Charmion smiled with an air of incredulity. "That shouldn't cause you much grief; for each of your glances pierces men's hearts like the golden arrows of Eros himself."

"Can a queen," went on Cleopatra, "know if it is the diadem or the brow beneath that is loved in her? The beams of her sidereal crown dazzle men's eyes and hearts; were I to come down from the height of my throne, would I enjoy the celebrity and the popularity of Bacchide or Archenassa, of any chance courtesan from Athens or Miletus? A queen is something so far above men, something so lofty, so separated, so impossible! What presumption can flatter itself with hopes of success in such an enterprise? It is no longer a woman, it is an august and sacred figure that has no longer a sex, a being one adores on bended knees without loving, like the statue of a goddess. Who has ever been seriously in love with Hera of the snowy arms, with Pallas of the sea-green eyes? Who has ever tried to kiss the silver feet of Thetis, and the rosy fingers of Aurora? What lover of those divine beauties has ever taken wings to fly towards the golden palaces of heaven? Respect and terror freeze men's souls in our presence, and to be loved by our equals we must needs descend, to the cities of the dead that I was talking of just now."

Although she put forward no objection to the reasoning of her mistress, a vague smile flitting about the lips of the Greek slave showed that she had no great belief in this inviolability of the royal person.

"Ah," continued Cleopatra, "I would like something to happen to me, a strange adventure, something unexpected. The song of the poets, the dance of the Syrian slaves, feasts crowned with roses and prolonged till daybreak, midnight races, Laconian dogs, tame lions, humpbacked dwarfs, members of the fellowship of the inimitable, combats in the circus, and ornaments, robes of byssus, matched strings of pearls, perfumes of Asia, the most exquisite elegances, the most senseless sumptuousness, nothing amuses me anymore: everything is indifferent to me, everything is insupportable!"

"It is obvious," murmured Charmion, "that the queen hasn't had a lover or killed anybody for a month."

Tired by such a long outburst, Cleopatra lifted again the cup placed beside her, moistened her lips in it, and, putting her head under her arm with a dovelike movement, settled herself as comfortably as possible to sleep. Charmion undid her sandals, and began softly to tickle the soles of her feet with the feathers of a peacock's quill; sleep did not tarry in flinging its golden powder over the lovely eyes of the sister of Ptolemy.

While Cleopatra is sleeping, let us mount again to the bridge of the cange, and enjoy the wonderful spectacle of the setting sun. A wide band of violet, strongly warmed by reddish tones towards the west, fills all the lower part of the sky; as it meets the azure zones, the violet tint melts into clear lilac, and is drowned in the blue in a half shade of rose; on the side where the sun, red like a buckler fallen from Vulcan's furnace, throws burning reflected light, the shades turn to pale lemon, and produce tints like those of turquoises. The water, rippled by an oblique beam, had the flat radiance of a mirror seen from the foil, or a damascened blade; the windings of the river, the reeds, and all the undulations of the bank stand out in firm black lines, which the whitish reflections throw into strong relief. Thanks to this twilight clarity you will see down there, like a grain of dust fallen on quicksilver, a little brown point which trembles in a network of shining threads. Is it a teal that is diving, a tortoise letting itself drift on the stream, a crocodile raising the end of his scaly snout to breathe the less burning evening air, the stomach of a hippopotamus stretching himself on the water's surface? or else indeed a rock left uncovered by the lowering of the river? for the old Hopi-Mou, Father of the Waters, has indeed need to fill his exhausted urn at the rains of the solstice in the Mountains of the Moon.

It is none of these. By the fragments of Osiris so happily sewn together! it is a man who seems to be walking and skating on the water; now the skiff that bears him can be seen, a real nutshell, a hollowed out fish, three bands of cork fitted together, one for the bottom and two for the sides, the whole solidly tied at the two ends by a cord daubed with bitumen. A man is standing upright, one foot on each side of this frail contrivance, which he guides by a single oar that serves at the same time as rudder, and although the royal cange flies rapidly along under the power of fifty oars, the little black skiff gains visibly upon it.

Cleopatra was wanting some strange incident, something unexpected; this little slim skiff, with its mysterious behavior, has in our eyes all the appearance of bringing, if not an adventure, at least an adventurer. Perhaps it contains the hero of our story; the thing is not impossible.

It was, in any case, a handsome young man of twenty, with hair so black that it seemed blue, a skin fair as gold, and proportions so perfect that one would have said a bronze of Lysippus; although he had been rowing a long time, he betrayed no sign of fatigue, and on his brow was not a single bead of sweat.

The sun plunged beneath the horizon, and on its jagged disk was drawn the brown silhouette of a distant city that the eye could barely have discovered without this trick of lighting; soon it went down altogether, and the stars, those evening flowering blossoms of the night, opened their golden calices to the azure firmament. The royal cange, followed closely by the little skiff, stopped near a stairway of black marble, each step of which was supported by one of the sphinxes hated by Cleopatra. It was the landing stage of the summer palace.

Cleopatra, leaning on Charmion, passed rapidly like a glittering vision, between a double row of slaves carrying signal torches.

The young man took from the bottom of the boat a large lion skin, threw it on his shoulders, leaped lightly to the ground, drew the skiff up the steep bank, and made his way towards the palace.

III

Who is this young man who, standing on a bit of cork, dares to follow the royal cange, and who can race against fifty rowers of the country of Kush, naked to the waist, and rubbed with palm tree oil? What motive urges him on and rouses his activity? That is what we are obliged to know in our quality of a poet gifted with the gift of intuition, for whom all men, and even all women, and that is more difficult, should have in their sides the window which Momus craved.

It is maybe not very easy to re-create the thoughts some two thousand years ago, of a young man of the land of Keme who followed the bark of Cleopatra, Queen and Goddess Euergetes, returning from the Mammisi of Hermonthis. We shall attempt it all the same.

Ammon, son of Mandouschopsh, was a young man of a strange character: nothing that touched the common run of mortals made any impression on him; he seemed of a higher race, and one might have named him the product of some divine adultery. His look had the radiance and the fixity of the sparrow-hawk's, and serene majesty sat on his brow as on a marble pedestal; a noble disdain arched his upper lip, and swelled his nostrils like those of a spirited steed; though he had almost the delicate grace of a young girl, and though Dionysus, that effeminate god, had not a more rounded or polished chest, he hid under this soft exterior nerves of steel and Herculean strength, that singular privilege of certain ancient natures of uniting the beauty of the woman with the strength of the man.

As to his color, we are obliged to admit that he was tawny as an orange, a color opposed to the white and rose idea we have of beauty; but that did not prevent him from being a very charming young man, much sought after by all sorts of women, yellow, red, copper-colored, swarthy, golden, and even by more than one white Greek.

After that, don't go and imagine that Ammon was a lady-killer; the ashes of old Priam, the snows of Hippolytus himself were not more insensible or cold; the young neophyte in his white tunic, getting ready for the initiation to the mysteries of Isis, does not lead a more chaste life; the young girl who passes by in the glacial shadow of her mother has not his fearful purity.

The pleasures of Ammon, for a young man of such a shy temperament, were all the same of a singular nature; he set out tranquilly in the morning with his little buckler of hippopotamus hide, his harpe or saber with a curved blade, his triangular bow and his quiver of serpent skin filled with barbed arrows; then he plunged into the desert, and set his mare, with her lean legs, her straight head, her disheveled mane, to the gallop till he found the track of a lioness; it gave him great enjoyment to go and take the little lion cubs from under their mother's body. In everything he loved only the perilous or the impossible; he delighted in walking by impracticable paths, or swimming in raging waters, and he would have chosen for a bathe in the Nile precisely the spot where the cataracts are; the abyss called him.

Such was Ammon, son of Mandouschopsh.

For some time back his humor had become ever more unsociable; he buried himself for months at a time in the ocean of sand and only reappeared at rare intervals. His anxious mother hung vainly over the top of her terrace and questioned the road with a tireless eye. After a long wait, a little cloud of dust eddied on the horizon; soon the cloudburst and revealed Ammon covered with dust, on his mare, who was as thin as a wolf, her eye red and bloodshot, her nostrils trembling, with scars on her side, scars which were not the marks of the spur.

After having hung up in his room some hyena or lion skin, he set out again.

And yet no one could have been happier than Ammon; he was loved by Naphe, the daughter of the priest Afomouthis, the most beautiful girl in the nome of Arsine. One would have to be Ammon not to see that Naphe had charming eyes tilted at the corners with an indefinable expression of voluptuousness, a mouth round which sparkled a rosy smile, clear white teeth, arms exquisitely rounded, and feet more perfect than the jasper feet of the statue of Isis; assuredly there was not in all Egypt a smaller hand or longer hair. The charms of Naphe could have been surpassed only by those of Cleopatra. But who could dream of loving Cleopatra? Ixion, who was in love with Juno, clasped in his arms only a cloud, and he turns forever on his wheel among the shades.

It was Cleopatra that Ammon loved!

He had at first tried to subdue this mad passion, he had struggled in hand-to-hand fight against it; but love is not throttled as one throttles a lion, and the most vigorous athletes can do nothing about it. The arrow was stuck in the wound and he dragged it about with him everywhere; the picture of Cleopatra, radiant and splendid under her diadem with golden points, standing alone in her imperial purple among a kneeling people, glittered in his waking moments and in his dreams; like a rash man who has looked at the sun and who sees always an intangible spot flicker before him, Ammon saw always Cleopatra. Eagles can contemplate the sun without being dazzled, but what eyeball of diamond can be fixed with impunity on a beautiful woman, on a beautiful queen?

His life consisted in wandering round the royal dwellings so as to breathe the same air as Cleopatra, so as to kiss on the sand – a felicity, alas! too rare – the half effaced imprint of her foot; he followed the sacred feasts and the panegyries, trying to snatch a beam from her eyes, to steal in passing one of the thousand aspects of her beauty. Sometimes shame came upon him at this senseless existence; he gave himself up to hunting with a redoubled fury, and tried to subdue by fatigue the heat of his blood and the tumult of his desires.

He had gone to the panegyry of Hermonthis, and, in the vague hope of seeing the queen again for an instant, when she disembarked at the summer palace, he had followed the cange in his skiff, without heeding the bitter stings of the sun in a heat enough to melt in lava-sweat the sphinxes panting on their reddened pedestals.

And then he understood that he had come to a supreme moment, that his life was about to be decided, and that he could not die with his secret in his heart.

It is a strange situation to love a queen; it is as if one loved a star, and still the star comes each night to shine in its place in the sky; it is a kind of mysterious rendezvous; you find her there, you see her, she is not angry at you for looking at her! Oh, misery! to be poor, unknown, obscure, seated at the very bottom of the ladder, and to feel your heart full of love for something solemn, sparkling, and splendid, for a woman whose meanest servant would have nothing to do with you! to have your eyes fixed on someone who does not see you, who will never see you, for whom you are nothing but a figure in the crowd like all the other figures, and who would meet you a hundred times without recognizing you! to have, if ever the opportunity for speaking arises, no reason to give for such a crazy audacity, neither a poet's talent, nor great genius, nor superhuman qualities, nothing but love; and in exchange for beauty, nobility, power, all the splendors of your dreams, to bring only passion or your youth, rare things indeed!

These ideas oppressed Ammon; lying prone on the sand, his chin on his hands, he let himself be carried away and uplifted on the flood of a never-failing reverie; he sketched out a thousand plans, each more insensate than the other. He realized quite clearly that he was striving for an impossible end, but he had not the courage to renounce it frankly, and perfidious hope came whispering at his ear some lying promise.

"Hathor, powerful goddess," he said in a low voice, "what have I done to you that you make me so unhappy! Are you avenging yourself for the disdain that I have for Naphe, the daughter of the priest Afomouthis? Are you angry with me for having repulsed Lamia, the hetaira of Athens, or Flora, the courtesan from Rome? Is it my fault if my heart is susceptible to the beauty of Cleopatra alone, your rival? Why have you sunk in my soul the poisoned arrows of impossible love? What sacrifices and what offerings do you demand? Must I raise a chapel of the rose marble of Syene with columns and gilded capitals, a ceiling in one piece, and hollow sculptured hieroglyphics by the best workmen of Memphis or Thebes? Answer me."

Like all the gods and goddesses that man invokes, Hathor answered nothing. Ammon made a desperate resolve.

Cleopatra, on her side, also invoked the goddess Hathor; she asked of her a new pleasure, an unknown sensation; languidly lying on her bed, she mused that the number of senses is very limited, that the most exquisite refinements are very quickly followed by disgust, and that a queen has really a lot of trouble to fill in her day. Trying poisons on slaves, making men fight with tigers, or gladiators with one another, drinking melted pearls, squandering a province, all that is pointless and ordinary.

Charmion was reduced to her last expedient, and didn't know what to make of her mistress.

All at once a whizzing was heard, an arrow came and planted itself quivering in the cedar facing of the wall.

Cleopatra almost fainted with terror. Charmion rushed to the window, and only saw a flake of foam on the river. A roll of papyrus surrounded the wooden shaft of the arrow; it contained these words written in phonetic characters: "I love you!"

IV

"I love you," repeated Cleopatra, twisting between her frail white fingers the bit of papyrus rolled up like a scytale, "that is the message I was asking for; what intelligent soul, what hidden genius has understood my desire so well?"

And thoroughly aroused from her languid torpor, she jumped down from her bed with the agility of a cat who scents a mouse, put her little ivory feet in her embroidered tatbebs, threw her byssus tunic over her shoulders, and ran to the window through which Charmion was still looking.

The night was clear and serene: the moon had already risen and sketched with great angles of light and shade the architectural masses of the palace, standing out boldly on a background of bluish transparency, and freezing to watered silver the water of the river in which its reflection streamed in a gleaming column; a light puff of wind, which could have been taken for the breath of the sleeping sphinxes, fluttered the reeds and set the azure bells of the lotus trembling; the cables of the small boats moored to the banks of the Nile groaned feebly, and the flood complained on its bed like a dove without its mate. A vague perfume of vegetation, sweeter than that of the aromatics that burn in the anschir of the priests of Anubis, drifted into the room. It was one of those enchanted nights of the East, more splendid than our most beautiful days, for our sun does not compare with that moon.

"Don't you see down there, almost in the middle of the river, a man's head swimming? Look now, he is crossing the track of light, and is being lost in the shadow: he can't be seen any longer." And, resting on Charmion's shoulder, she leaned half her beautiful body out of the window to try to find again the track of the mysterious swimmer. But a clump of Nile acacias, of doums and sayals, threw at that spot its shadow on the river and protected the flight of the audacious man. If Ammon had had the good wit to turn round, he would have seen Cleopatra, the sidereal queen, looking greedily for him across the night, for him, poor obscure Egyptian that he was, a wretched hunter of lions.

"Charmion! Charmion! bid Phrehipephbour, the chief of the rowers, come, and tell them to launch without delay two boats in pursuit of that man," said Cleopatra, whose curiosity was excited to the highest degree.

Phrehipephbour appeared; he was a man of the race of the Nahasi, with broad hands, muscular arms, wearing a cap of a red color on his head, rather like a Phrygian helmet, and clothed in a tight pair of drawers, striped diagonally white and blue. His bust, entirely bare, shone in the light of the lamp, black and polished like a ball of jade. He took the queen's orders and retired at once to execute them.

Two long barks, narrow, so light that the slightest forgetfulness of equilibrium must have capsized them, cleft at once the waters of the Nile, whistling under the strength of twenty vigorous rowers, but the search was useless. After having beaten the river in all directions, after having ransacked the smallest tuft of reeds, Phrehipephbour returned to the palace without any other result but that of having raised some heron, asleep erect on one leg, or troubled some crocodile in his digestion.

Cleopatra experienced such a strong resentment at this rebuff that she had a great desire to condemn Prehipephbour to the grindstone or the beasts. Fortunately Charmion interceded for the wretch, who was all in a panic, paling with fear under his black skin. It was the only time in her life that one of her desires had not been granted as soon as formulated; so she felt an uneasy surprise, like a first doubt of her all-powerfulness.

She, Cleopatra, wife and sister of Ptolemy, proclaimed Goddess Euergetes, reigning Queen of the Lands Below and Above, Eye of the Sky, the Favorite of the Sun, as can be seen on the cartouches sculptured on the walls of temples, to meet an obstacle, to wish a thing that was not done, to have spoken and not been obeyed! One might as well be the wife of some poor paraschist who incised dead bodies, and melt soda in a kettle! It is monstrous, it is exorbitant, and one must be, in truth, a very kind and very clement queen, not to crucify this wretched Phrehipephbour.

You were wanting an adventure, something strange and unexpected; you have got just what you wished. You see that your realm is not so dead as you claimed. It is no stone arm from a statue that has sped that arrow, it is not from the heart of a mummy that these three words which have moved you so have come, you who see with a smile on your lips your poisoned slaves beating with their heels and their heads in the convulsions of agony your beautiful mosaic and porphyry pavements, you who applaud the tiger when he has stoutly buried his jaws in the side of a conquered gladiator.

You will have all that you wish, cars of silver starred with emeralds, four-wheeled chariots of griffins, tunics of thrice dyed purple, mirrors of steel framed with precious stones, so clear that you can see yourself therein as lovely as you are; robes come from the lands of the East, so fine, so thin that they can pass through the ring of your little finger; pearls of a perfect water, goblets wrought by Lysippus or Myron, parrots from India that speak like poets; you will get everything, even if you demand the cestus of Venus, or the pschent of Isis; but, in very truth, you will not have this evening the man who shot that arrow that trembles still in the cedar wood of your bed.

The slaves who will dress you tomorrow will have no easy task; they will be well advised to have a light hand; the golden toilet pins might well have for sheath the throat of the clumsy hair-waver, and the depilator runs a strong risk of being hung up to the ceiling by her feet.

"Who could have had the audacity to shoot that declaration fitted to an arrow? Is it the monarch Amoun-Ra who thinks himself handsomer than the Grecian Apollo? What do you think of him, Charmion? Or rather Cheapsiro, the commandant of Hermothybria, so proud of his combats in the country of Kush! Wouldn't it rather be young Sextus, the Roman debauchee who puts on rouge, rolls his r's in speaking and wears sleeves in the Persian mode?"

"Queen, it is none of these; although you are the loveliest lady in the world, these men flatter you and do not love you. The monarch Amoun-Ra has chosen an idol to whom he will always be faithful, and that is his own person; the warrior Cheapsiro, thinks only of relating his battles; as to Sextus, he is so seriously occupied with the composition of a new cosmetic that he can think of nothing else. Besides he has received some overcoats from Laconia, yellow tunics embroidered with gold, and some Asiatic children who are absorbing him entirely. None of these fine gentlemen would risk his neck in an enterprise so rash and so perilous; they do not love you enough for that.

"You were saying in your cange that dazzled eyes never dared aspire to you, and that men could only pale and fall at your feet asking pardon, and that there remained for you no other resource than to waken in his gilded coffin some old Pharaoh perfumed with bitumen. Now there is an ardent young heart which loves you. What will you do with it?"

That night Cleopatra had difficulty in sleeping; she turned on her bed, she called long in vain on Morpheus, brother of Death; she repeated several times that she was the most unhappy of queens, that everyone made it their business to thwart her, and that her life was unendurable; huge grievances which affected Charmion rather lightly, though she put on an expression of sympathy with them.

Let us leave Cleopatra for a little, seeking the sleep that flies from her, and running over in her conjectures all the nobles of the court; let us go back to Ammon. More skillful than Phrehipephbour the chief of the rowers, we shall certainly succeed in finding him.

Terrified by his own hardihood, Ammon flung himself into the Nile, and had reached swimming the little clump of doum-palms before Phrehipephbour had launched the two barks in pursuit.

When he had got back his breath, and pushed behind his ears his long black hair, soaked with the foam of the river, he felt calmer and more at ease. Cleopatra had something which came from him. A connection existed between them now; Cleopatra was thinking of him, Ammon. Maybe it was a thought of wrath, but at least he had succeeded in arousing in her some sort of feeling, terror, anger, or pity; he had made her recognize his existence. It is true that he had forgotten to put his name on the strip of papyrus; but what more would the name convey to the queen; Ammon, son of Mandouschopsch!

A monarch or a slave were equal before her. A goddess does not abase herself more in taking as a lover a man of the people than a patrician or a king; from such a height nothing is seen in a man but his love.

The sentence that had been weighing on his breast like the knee of a bronze colossus, had at length emerged; it had crossed the air, it had arrived as far as the queen, the point of the triangle, the inaccessible summit! In that blasé soul it had set curiosity, an immense progress.

Ammon did not suspect that he had succeeded so well, but he was more tranquil, for he had sworn to himself by the mystic Bari, who guards the souls in Amenthi; by the sacred birds, Bennon and Ghenghen; by Typhon and by Osiris; by every formidable name that Egyptian mythology could offer, that he would be the lover of Cleopatra, were it only for a day, were it only for a night, were it only for an hour, though it cost him his body and his soul.

How this love had come upon him for a woman that he had seen only from afar, and to whom he scarcely dared to raise his eyes, he who did not drop them before the yellow eyeballs of the lions, and how this little seed fallen by chance in his soul had sprung up there so quickly and thrown out such deep roots, is a mystery that we shall not explain; we have said above: the abyss called him.

When he was quite sure that Phrehipephbour had gone in with his rowers, he flung himself a second time in the Nile, and made his way again to the palace of Cleopatra whose lamp shone through a purple curtain, and seemed a painted star. Leander did not swim towards the tower of Sestos with more courage and vigor, and yet Ammon was not waited for by a Hero ready to pour on his head jars of perfumes to banish the odors of the sea, and the bitter kisses of the tempest.

Some shrewd blow of a lance or harpe was all that could happen to him at the best, and to tell the truth, it was hardly that of which he was afraid.

He skirted for some time the wall of the palace, whose marble feet bathed in the river, and stopped before a submerged opening, through which the water rushed in whirlpools. He dived two or three times unsuccessfully; at last he was more fortunate, hit on the passage and disappeared.

This arcade was a vaulted canal which led the waters of the Nile to Cleopatra's baths.

V

Cleopatra only fell asleep in the morning, at the hour when the dreams return that have flitted through the ivory gate. The illusion of sleep led her to see all sorts of lovers, swimming across rivers, clambering up walls to reach her, and, in memory of the night before, her dreams were riddled with arrows charged with declarations of love. Her little heels, fluttering in agitation, struck the breast of Charmion sleeping across the bed to serve as her cushion.

When she awoke, a gay sunbeam played in the window curtain, the web of which it pierced with a thousand points of light, and came familiarly to the bed to flit like a golden butterfly round her lovely shoulders which it skimmed in passing with a luminous kiss. Happy sunbeam that the gods might have envied!

Cleopatra asked to get up in an expiring voice like a sick child's; two of her women raised her in their arms and laid her preciously on the ground on a huge tiger skin whose claws were of gold and whose eyes were carbuncles. Charmion wrapped her in a calasiris of linen whiter than milk, and put her feet in tatbebs of cork on the soles of which had been drawn, in token of contempt, two grotesque figures representing two men of the races of Nahasi and Nahmou, bound hand and foot, so that Cleopatra deserved literally the epithet of "she who treads on the peoples" which the royal cartouches give her.

It was the hour for the bath. Cleopatra went there with her women.

Cleopatra's baths were built in vast gardens filled with mimosas, carob trees, aloes, lemon trees, Persian apple trees, the luxuriant freshness of which made a delicious contrast with the sterility of the surroundings; immense terraces sustained groves of verdure, and raised the flowers up to the sky by gigantic stairways of rose granite; vases of Pentelic marble spread like huge lilies on the side of each step, and the plants they contained, seemed only their pistils; chimeras caressed by the chisels of the most able Greek sculptors, of a less repulsive appearance than the Egyptian sphinxes with their surly faces and their morose attitudes, were lying at ease on the turf all studded with flowers, like graceful white greyhounds on a drawing room carpet; there were charming figures of women, their noses straight, their foreheads smooth, their mouths little, their arms delicately rounded, their throats round and pure, with ear-pendants, collars, and ornaments, capricious and adorable, bifurcating into a fish's tail like the woman of whom Horace spoke, unfurling on the wings of a bird, widening into the flanks of a lioness, twisting into a volute of foliage, according to the fantasy of the artist or the suitability of the architectural position: a double row of these delicious monsters bordered the alley that led from the palace to the bath-chamber.

At the end of this alley a large swimming pool was reached with four stairways of porphyry; through the transparency of the crystalline water the steps could be seen going down to the bottom sanded with powdered gold; women, ending in sheaths like caryatides, spouted from their breasts a stream of perfumed water, which fell into the pool in a silver dew, dimpling the clear mirror with little crackling drops. In addition to this use the caryatides had in addition the other of supporting on their heads an entablature adorned with Nereids and tritons in bas-relief and supplied with a bronze ring to which to attach the silken cords of the awning. Beyond the gateway was seen greenery, damp and blue-tinted, shady bowers of coolness, a bit of the vale of Tempe transplanted into Egypt. The famous gardens of Semiramis were nothing compared to these.

We shall not speak of the seven or eight other chambers at different temperatures, with their hot and cold vapors, their boxes of perfume, their cosmetics, their oils, their pumice-stone, their horsehair gloves, and all the refinements of the ancient art of bathing pushed to such a high degree of voluptuousness and luxury.

Cleopatra arrived, her hand on Charmion's shoulder; she had walked at least thirty steps alone! a mighty effort! an enormous fatigue! A slight shade of rose, spreading under the transparent skin of her cheeks, freshened their passionate pallor; on her temples, fair as amber, was seen a network of blue veins; her level brow, low like the brows of the olden times, but perfect in its roundness and form, joined by an irreproachable line to a severe straight nose, like a cameo, intersected by rosy nostrils that palpitated at the least emotion like the nostrils of a tigress in love; the little mouth, round, very close to the nose, had its lip scornfully arched; but an unbridled voluptuousness, an incredible ardor for life, gleamed in the red splendor and the moist luster of the lower lip. Her eyes had straight lids, the eyebrows narrow and almost without inflection. We shall not try to give an idea of them; it was a fire, a languor, a glittering limpidity, enough to turn the head of Anubis' dog himself; each look of her eyes was a poem finer than that of Homer or Mimnermus; an imperial chin, full of force and domination, worthily finished off this charming profile.

She stood erect on the first step of the pool, in an attitude full of grace and pride; slightly curving backwards, her foot raised like a goddess about to quit her pedestal whose eyes are still in the sky. Two superb folds hung from the points of her bosom, and flowed in a single line of the ground. Cleomenes, if he had been her contemporary, and if he could have seen her, would have broken his Venus in pieces in disgust.

Before entering the water, touched by a new whim, she asked Charmion to change her headdress of silver net; she wanted rather a crown of lotus flowers and reeds, like a sea goddess. Charmion obeyed, her hair flowed free, and fell in black cascades on her shoulders, and hung in clusters like ripe grapes along her lovely cheeks.

Then the linen tunic, held only by a golden brooch, was loosened, slipped down her marble body, and lay collapsed in a white cloud at her feet like the swan at the feet of Leda.

And Ammon, where was he?

Oh, cruelty of fate! So many insensible objects were enjoying favors that would ravish a lover with joy. The wind that plays with perfumed locks or gives to fair lips kisses which it cannot appreciate, the water which is absolutely indifferent to this voluptuousness, and which covers with a single caress the lovely adored body, the mirror which reflects so many charming pictures, the cothurnus or the tatbeb which encloses a divine little foot; ah! how many lost happinesses!

Cleopatra dipped her vermilion heel in the water, and descended several steps; the trembling water made her a girdle and bracelet of silver, and rolled in pearls on her breast and shoulders like an unstrung necklace; her long hair, uplifted by the water, spread behind her like a royal mantle: she was queen even in the bath. She came and went, diving and bringing up in her hands from the bottom handfuls of powdered gold which she threw laughing to some of her women; at other times she hung from the balustrade of the pool hiding and revealing her treasures, now letting no more than her polished, lustrous back be seen, now showing herself complete like Venus Anadyomene and varying ceaselessly the aspects of her beauty.

Suddenly she uttered a cry more sharp than that of Diana surprised by Acteon; she had seen through the foliage a burning eyeball gleam, yellow and phosphorescent like the eye of a crocodile or of a lion.

It was Ammon who, crouching on the earth, behind a tuft of leaves, more breathless then a fawn among the corn, was growing intoxicated with the dangerous good fortune of seeing the queen in her bath. Though he was courageous to the extent of temerity, the cry of Cleopatra entered his heart colder than the blade of a sword: a mortal sweat covered all his body; his arteries beat in his temples with a strident noise; the iron hand of anxiety pressed his throat and stifled him.

The eunuchs ran up, lance in hand. Cleopatra showed them the group of trees where they found Ammon, squat and cowering on the ground. Defense was impossible; he did not attempt it, and let himself be taken. They got ready to kill him with the cruel and stupid impassibility which characterizes eunuchs; but Cleopatra, who had had time to wrap herself in her calasiris, signed to them with her hand to stop and to bring the prisoner to her.

Ammon could only fall on his knees and stretch out suppliant hands to her as to the altar of the gods.

"Are you some assassin bribed by Rome; and what do you come to do in these sacred grounds where men are forbidden?" said Cleopatra with an imperious gesture of interrogation.

"May my soul be found light in the balances of Amenthi, and may Yme, daughter of the Sun and goddess of Truth, punish me if ever I had against you, O Queen, an evil thought," answered Ammon, still on his knees.

Sincerity and loyalty shone on his face in characters so transparent that Cleopatra immediately abandoned this thought, and fixed on the young Egyptian a less severe and irritated look; she found him handsome.

"Well, then, what reason drove you to a place where you could meet nothing but death?"

"I love you," said Ammon in a low voice but distinctly; for his courage came back, as it does in all extreme situations which nothing can make worse.

"Ah!" said Cleopatra, leaning towards him and seizing his arm with a brusque and sudden movement. "It is you who shot the arrow with the papyrus roll; by Oms, the god of the lower world, you are a very daring wretch! I recognize you now; for a long time I have seen you wandering like a plaintive shade round the spots I inhabit. You were at the procession of Isis, at the panegyry of Hermonthis; you followed the royal cange. Ah! you must have a queen! You have no mediocre ambitions; you expected doubtless to have your reward at once. Certainly I am going to love you. Why not?"

"Queen," answered Ammon with an air of grave melancholy, "do not jest. I am out of my wits, it is true. I have deserved death, that is true too; be human, kill me."

"No, I have the whim to be merciful today. I give you your life."

"What do you expect me to do with life? I love you."

"Well! you shall be satisfied; you shall die," answered Cleopatra. "You have dreamed a strange extravagant dream; your desires have passed in imagination an unapproachable threshold, you thought that you were Cesar or Mark Antony; you loved the queen! In certain hours of delirium you have believed that in the suite of circumstances that occur only once in a thousand years, Cleopatra would one day love you. Well, what you believed impossible is going to be accomplished; I am going to make your dream a reality; it pleases me, for once, to crown a mad hope. It is my wish to flood you with splendor, with sunbeams and lightning. It is my wish that your fortune be dazzling. You were at the bottom of the wheel, I am going to put you on top, brusquely, suddenly, without transition. I take you from nothingness: I make you the equal of a god, and I replunge you into nothingness; that's all, but do not come to me and call me cruel, implore my pity; do not weaken when the hour strikes. I am kind, I lend myself to your folly; I would have the right to have you killed at once; but you say that you love me; I shall have you killed tomorrow; your life for a night. I am generous, I buy it from you, I could have taken it. But what are you doing at my feet? Rise and give me your hand to go into the palace."

VI

Our world is indeed small beside the old world, our feats are shabby beside the fearful sumptuousness of the Roman patricians and the princes of Asia; their ordinary meals would pass today for unlicensed orgies, and the whole of a modern city would live for a week on the dessert of Lucullus when he supped with some intimate friends. We, with our miserable habits, have difficulty in conceiving those enormous existences, that realized all recklessness, strangeness, and the most monstrous impossibilities that the imagination can invent. Our palaces are stables where Caligula would not have wanted to stable his horse; the richest of our constitutional kings does not keep up the state of a petty satrap or a Roman proconsul. The radiant suns that shone on the earth are forever extinguished in the nothingness of uniformity; there rise no more on the black ant-heap of men those colossi in Titan's shape who crossed the world in three steps like Homer's horses; there are no more towers of Lylacq, no more giant Babels scaling the sky with infinite spirals, no more inordinate temples made with quarters of mountains, or royal terraces that each century and each people can only raise one layer higher, whence the prince, leaning meditatively on his elbow, can see the whole face of the world like an unrolled map; no more of those confused cities, composed of an inextricable heap of Cyclopean edifices, with their deep circumvallations, their circuses bellowing night and day, their reservoirs filled with seawater, and peopled with leviathans and whales, their colossal flights of stairs, their superimposed terraces, their towers with the coping bathed in clouds, their giant palaces, their aqueducts, their heaving cities and their gloomy necropolises! Alas, nothing more than hives of plaster are left us on a checkerboard of paving-stones!

People are astonished that men did not revolt against these confiscations of all the wealth and all the living force to the profit of a certain few privileged people, and that such exorbitant fantasies did not meet obstacles on their bloody way. The reason is, that these prodigious existences were the realization under the sun of the dream that all of us dream at night; the personification of the common thought, and that the people saw themselves living in symbol under one of these meteoric names which blaze inextinguishably in the night of the ages. Today, deprived of this glowing spectacle of the all-powerful will, of this high contemplation of a human soul whose slightest desire is translated into unheard-of actions, into granite and bronze enormities, the world is absolutely and desperately bored; mankind is no longer represented in its imperial fantasy.

The story we are writing, and the great name of Cleopatra which figures in it, have plunged us into those reflections which displease a civilized ear. But the spectacle of the ancient world is something so overwhelming, so discouraging for imaginations that believe themselves unlicensed, and for spirits that imagine they have attained the last limits of fairylike magnificence, that we could not refrain from registering here our complaints and regrets that we were not contemporary with Sardanapalus, with Tiglath-Pileser, with Cleopatra, Queen of Egypt, or even of Heliogabalus, Emperor of Rome and Priest of the Sun.

We have to describe a supreme orgy, a feast that threw Belshazzar's into the shade, a night with Cleopatra. How, in the French language, so chaste, so glacially prude, shall we describe this frantic outburst, this mighty, powerful debauch that was not afraid to mingle blood and wine, those two purples, and the furious transports of unsatisfied voluptuousness rushing to the impossible; all the fervor of the senses which the long fast of Christianity has not yet subdued?

The promised night must be a splendid one; it was necessary that all the possible joys of a human existence should be concentrated into a few hours; it was necessary to make of Ammon's life a potent elixir which he might drain in a single cup. Cleopatra wished to dazzle her voluntary victim, and to plunge him in a whirlpool of heady pleasures, to intoxicate him, to madden him with the wine of the orgy, so that death, although accepted, should come without being seen or comprehended.

Let us carry our readers into the banquet-hall.

Our present-day architecture offers few points of comparison with those immense buildings whose ruins bear more resemblance to the landslip of a mountain than to the debris of houses. It requires all the exaggeration of ancient life to people and fill those prodigious palaces whose rooms were so vast that they could have no other ceiling than the sky; a magnificent ceiling, and one well worthy of such architecture!

The banquet-hall had enormous Babylonian proportions; the eye could not penetrate its incommensurable depth! monstrous columns, short, squat, solid enough to support the pole, spread heavily out their splayed shafts on pedestals covered with many-colored hieroglyphics, and sustained on their big-bellied capitals gigantic arcades of granite, advancing by layers like steps set upside-down. Between each pillar a colossal sphinx of basalt, topped by a pschent, stretched out its head with oblique eyes and horned chin, and cast on the hall a fixed mysterious gaze. On the second story, behind the first, the capitals of the columns, slimmer than the first, were replaced by four heads of women placed back to back, with the fluted lappets and the twists of the Egyptian headdress; instead of sphinxes, idols with bull heads, impassive spectators of the nocturnal delirium and the orgiastic revels, were seated in seats of stone like patient guests who are waiting till the feast begins.

A third stage of a different order, with bronze elephants shooting scented water from their trunks, crowned the building; above that the sky opened like a blue gulf, and the curious stars leant over the frieze.

Prodigious stairways of porphyry, so polished that they reflected the body like a mirror, rose up and down in all directions and linked these huge masses of architecture together.

We are only tracing here a rapid sketch to give an idea of the composition of this formidable erection with its proportions beyond all human measure. It would require the brush of Martin, the great painter of vanished mightiness, and we have only a thin penstroke in place of the apocalyptic depth of the black style; but the imagination will fill the void; less lucky than the painter and the musician, we can only present objects one after another. We have only spoken of the banqueting-hall, leaving aside the guests: and at that, we have done no more than indicate it. Cleopatra and Ammon are waiting us; here they come.

Ammon was clothed in a linen tunic studded with stars, with a purple mantle and bands in his hair like an Oriental king. Cleopatra wore a pale sea-green robe, split at the side, and kept together by golden bees; round her bare arms played two rows of large pearls; on her head gleamed the crown with golden points. In spite of the smile on her lips, a preoccupied shadow lightly brooded over her lovely forehead, and occasionally her eyebrows drew together in a feverish movement. What subject was it that could vex the great queen? As to Ammon, he had the glowing, shining look of a man in ecstasy or seeing visions; sparkling emanations, radiating from his temples and his brow, made him a golden halo, like to one of the twelve great gods of Olympus.

A grave profound joy shone on all his features; he had grasped his chimera of the restless wings, and it had not flown away; he had attained the object of his life. He might live to the age of Nestor or Priam; he might see his temples veined and covered with white hairs like those of the high priest of Ammon; he would experience nothing new, he would learn nothing further. He had been satisfied so abundantly beyond his maddest hopes that the world had nothing more to give him.

Cleopatra made him sit beside her on a throne flanked by golden griffins, and clapped her little hands together. Suddenly lines of fire, twinkling ropes, traced out the projections of the architecture: the eyes of the sphinxes emitted phosphorescent lights, a fiery breath came from the idols' jaws; the elephants, instead of perfumed water, spouted out a reddish jet; bronze arms sprang from the walls with torches in their hands; in the sculptured heart of the lotus expanded glittering plumes.

Broad bluish flames quivered in the brass tripods, giant candelabras shook their disheveled lights in a blazing mist; everything twinkled and glittered. Prismatic rainbows crossed and broke in the air; the facets of goblets, the angles of marbles and jaspers, the cut edges of vases became spangling, gleaming, or darting lights. Light flowed in torrents and fell from step to step like a waterfall on a stairway of porphyry; you would have said it was the reflection of a fire in a river; if the Queen of Sheba had stepped up there, she would have raised the hem of her dress, thinking she was walking on water as on Solomon's floor of glass. Through this shining fog, the monstrous figures of the colossi, the animals, the hieroglyphics seemed to move and live with a factitious life; the black granite rams grinned ironically and shook their golden horns, the idols breathed noisily through their panting nostrils.

The orgy was at its height; dishes of flamingos' tongues and parrot-fish liver, eels fattened on human flesh and prepared with garum, peacocks' brains, boars stuffed with living birds, and all the marvels of ancient feasts tenfold and a hundredfold, were heaped up on the three sections of the gigantic triclinium. Wines from Crete, from the Massicus and Falernum, foamed in golden bowls crowned with roses, filled by Asiatic pages whose beautiful floating hair served to wipe dry the hands of the guests. Musicians playing on the Egyptian timbrel, on the dulcimer, on the sambuca, and the harp of twenty-one strings, filled the upper balustrades and flung their harmonious rattle into the tempest of noise that floated round the feast; thunder would not have had a voice loud enough to make itself heard.

Ammon, his head leaning on Cleopatra's shoulder, felt his reason going from him; the banqueting-hall swayed round him like an immense architectural nightmare; he saw, through his bedazzlement, endless perspectives and colonnades; new zones of porticos were superimposed on the real ones, and soared into the skies to heights to which Babels have never attained. If he had not felt in his hand the soft cool hand of Cleopatra, he would have believed himself transported into a world of enchantment by a Thessalian sorcerer, or a Persian magician.

Towards the end of the repast, humpbacked dwarfs and morions executed grotesque dances and combats; the young Egyptian and Grecian girls, representing the black and the white hours, danced in the Ionian mode, a voluptuous dance performed with inimitable perfection.

Cleopatra herself rose from her throne, flung down her royal mantle, replaced her sidereal diadem by a garland of flowers, adjusted her golden castanets to her alabaster hands, and began to dance before Ammon, lost in ravishment. Her lovely arms, rounded like the handles of a marble vase, shook down above her head clusters of twinkling notes, and her castanets prattled with an ever-growing volubility. Raised on the vermilion tips of her little feet, she advanced quickly and came to brush the brow of Ammon with a kiss; then she recommenced her maneuvers and flitted round him, sometimes curving backwards, her head thrown back, her eyes half-closed, her arms swooning and dead, her hair unbound and hanging like a bacchante's on Mount Menalus swayed by her god; sometimes gay, alert, laughing, fluttering, tireless, and more capricious in her meanders than a pillaging bee. The love of the heart, the voluptuousness of the senses, ardent passion, inexhaustible fresh youth, the promise of approaching felicity, she expressed them all.

The shamefast stars looked no longer, their chaste golden eyeballs could not bear such a sight; the sky itself was hid, and a dome of inflamed mist covered the hall.

Cleopatra returned to seat herself near Ammon. The night wore on; the last of the black hours was about to fly away; the sky itself was hid; a bluish glimmer entered with perplexed step among this tumult of red lights, like a moonbeam that falls on a furnace: the high arcades grew softly blue; day was appearing.

Ammon took the horn vase that an Ethiopian slave of sinister aspect presented to him, a vase which contained a poison so potent that it would have shattered any other vessel. Throwing his life to his mistress in a last look, he carried to his lips the fatal cup where the poisoned liquor boiled and hissed.

Cleopatra grew pale, and put her hand on Ammon's arm to stay him. His courage touched her; she was going to say, "Live on to love me; I desire it," when the blast of bugles was heard. Four heralds at arms entered on horseback into the banqueting-hall. It was Mark Antony's officers who preceded their master by a few steps. Silently she dropped Ammon's arm. A sunbeam came to play on Cleopatra's forehead as if to replace her absent diadem.

"You see that the moment has come; it is the hour when lovely dreams fly away," said Ammon.

Then he drank at a single draft the fatal vase and fell as if struck by lightning. Cleopatra bent her head, and in the cup a burning tear, the only one she had shed in her life, went to join the melted pearl.

"By Hercules! my lovely queen, it was no use my making haste, I see that I have come too late," said Mark Antony, as he entered the banqueting-hall: "the supper is finished. But what is the meaning of this body lying on the flag-stones?"

"Oh, nothing," said Cleopatra, smiling. "It's a poison I was experimenting with to be ready for myself if Octavius took me a prisoner. Would it amuse you, my dear lord, to sit beside me and watch these Greek buffoons dance?"

The Fleece of Gold

I
TIBURCE

Tiburce was really a most extraordinary young man; his oddity had the peculiar merit of being unaffected; he did not lay it aside on returning home, as he did his hat and gloves; he was original between four walls, without spectators, for himself alone.

Do not conclude, I beg, that Tiburce was ridiculous, that he had one of those aggressive manias which are intolerable to all the world; he did not eat spiders, he played on no instrument, nor did he read poetry to anybody. He was a staid, placid youth, talking little, listening less; and his half-opened eyes seemed to be turned inward.

He passed his life reclining in the corner of a divan, supported on either side by a pile of cushions, worrying as little about the affairs of the time as about what was taking place in the moon. There were very few substantives which had-any effect on him, and no one was ever less susceptible to long words. He cared absolutely nothing for his political rights, and thought that the people were still free at the wine-shop.

His ideas on all subjects were very simple; he preferred to do nothing rather than to work; he preferred good wine to cheap wine and a beautiful woman to an ugly one; in natural history he made a classification – than which nothing could be more succinct; things that eat, and things that do not eat. In brief, he was absolutely detached from all human affairs, and was as reasonable as he appeared mad.

He had not the slightest self-esteem; he did not deem himself the pivot of creation, and realized fully that the world could turn without his assistance; he thought little more of himself than of the rind of a cheese, or of the eels in vinegar. In face of eternity and the infinite, he had not the courage to be vain; having looked sometimes through the microscope and the telescope, he had not an exaggerated idea of the importance of the human race. His height was five feet, four inches; but he said to himself that the people in the sun might well be eight hundred leagues tall.

Such was our friend Tiburce.

It would be a mistake to think from all this that Tiburce was devoid of passions. Beneath the ashes of that placid exterior smoldered more than one burning brand. However, no one knew of any regular mistress of his, and he displayed little gallantry toward women. Like almost all the young men of today, without being precisely a poet or a painter, he had read many novels and seen many pictures; lazy as he was, he preferred to live on the faith of other people; he loved with the poet's love, he looked with the eyes of the artist, and he was familiar with more poets than faces; reality was repugnant to him, and by dint of living in books and paintings, he had reached the point where nature no longer rang true.

The Madonnas of Raphael, the courtesans of Titian, caused the most celebrated beauties to seem ugly to him; Petrarch's Laura, Dante's Beatrice, Byron's Haides, Andre Chenier's Camille, threw completely into the shade the women in hats, gowns, and shoulder-capes whose lover he might have been. And yet he did not demand an ideal with white wings and a halo about her head; but his studies in antique statuary, the Italian schools, his familiarity with the masterpieces of art, and his reading of the poets had given him an exquisitely refined taste in the matter of form, and it would have been impossible for him to love the noblest mind on earth, unless it had the shoulders of the Venus of Milo. So it was that Tiburce was in love with no one.

His devotion to abstract beauty was manifested by the great number of statuettes, plaster casts, drawings and engravings with which his room and its walls were crowded, so that the ordinary bourgeois would have considered it rather an impossible abode; for he had no furniture save the divan mentioned above, and several cushions of different colors scattered over the carpet. Having no secrets, he could easily do without a secretary, and the incommodity of commodes was to him an established fact.

Tiburce rarely went into society, not from shyness, but from indifference; he welcomed his friends cordially, and never returned their visits. Was Tiburce happy? No; but he was not unhappy; he would have liked, however, to dress in red. Superficial persons accused him of insensibility, and kept women said that he had no heart; but in reality his was a heart of gold, and his search for physical beauty betrayed to observant eyes a painful disillusionment in the world of moral beauty. In default of sweetness of perfume, he sought grace in the vessel containing it; he did not complain, he indulged in no elegies, he did not wear ruffles en pleureuse; but one could see that he had suffered, that he had been deceived, and that he proposed not to love again except with his eyes open. As dissimulation of the body is much more difficult than dissimulation of the mind, he set much store by material perfection; but alas! a lovely body is as rare as a lovely soul. Moreover, Tiburce, depraved by the reflections of novel-writers, living in the charming, imaginary society created by poets, with his eyes full of the masterpieces of statuary and painting, had a lordly and scornful taste; and that which he took for love was simply the adoration of an artist. He found faults of drawing in his mistress; although he did not suspect it, woman was to him a model, nothing more.

One day, having smoked his hookah, having gazed at Correggio's threefold eda in its filleted frame, having turned Radine's latest statuette about in every direction, having taken his left foot in his right hand, and his right foot in his left hand, and having placed his sels on the edge of the mantel, Tiburce was forced to admit to himself that he had come to the end of his means of diversion, that he knew not which way to turn, and that the grey spiders of ennui were crawling down the walls of his room, all dusty with drowsiness.

He asked the time, and was told that it was a quarter to one, which seemed to him decisive and unanswerable. He bade his servant dress him and went out to walk the streets; as he walked he reflected that his heart was empty, and he felt the need of "making a passion," as they say in Parisian slang.

This laudable resolution formed, he propounded the following questions to himself: Shall I love a Spaniard with an amber complexion, frowning eyebrows, and jet-black hair? or an Italian with classic features, and orange-tinted eyelids encircling a glance of flame? or a slim-waisted Frenchwoman, with a nose a la Roxelane and a doll's foot? or a red Jewess with a sky-blue skin and green eyes? or a negress black as night, and gleaming like new bronze? Shall I have a fair or a dark passion? Terrible perplexity.

As he plodded along, head down, pondering this question, he ran against something hard, which caused him to jump back with a blood-curdling oath. That something was a painter friend of his; together they entered the Museum. The painter, an enthusiastic admirer of Rubens, paused by preference before the canvasses of the Dutch Michelangelo, whom he extolled with a most contagious frenzy of admiration. Tiburce, surfeited with the Greek outline, the Roman contour, the tawny tones of the Italian masters, took delight in the plump forms, the satiny flesh, the ruddy faces, as blooming as bouquets of flowers, the luxuriant health that the Antwerpian artist sends bounding through the veins of those faces of his, with their network of blue and scarlet. His eye caressed with sensuous pleasure those lovely pearl-white shoulders and those sirenlike hips drowned in waves of golden hair and marine pearls. Tiburce, who had an extraordinary faculty of assimilation, and who understood equally well the most contrasted types, was at that moment as Flemish as if he had been born in the polders and had never lost sight of Lillo fort and the steeples of Antwerp.

"It is decided," he said to himself as he left the gallery, "I will love a Fleming."

As Tiburce was the most logical person in the world, he placed before himself this irrefutable argument, namely, that Flemish women must be more numerous in Flanders than elsewhere, and that it was important for him to go to Belgium at once – to hunt the blonde. This Jason of a new type, in quest of another sort of gold, took the Brussels diligence that same evening, with the mad haste of a bankrupt weary of intercourse with men and feeling a craving to leave France, that classic home of the fine arts, of lovely women, and of sheriffs' officers.

After a few hours, Tiburce, not without a thrill of joy, saw the Belgian lion appear on the signs of inns, beneath a poodle in nankeen breeches, accompanied by the inevitable Verkoopt men dranken. On the following evening he walked on Magdalena Strass in Brussels, climbed the mountain with its kitchen gardens, admired the stained-glass windows of St. Gudule's and the belfry of the Hotel de Ville, and scrutinized, not without alarm, all the women who passed.

He met an incalculable number of Negresses, mulattresses, quadroons, half-breeds, griffs, yellow women, copper-colored women, green women, women of the color of a boot-flap, but not a single blonde; if it had been a little warmer he might have imagined himself at Seville; nothing was lacking, not even the black mantilla.

As he returned to his hotel on Rue d'Or, however, he saw a girl who was only a dark chestnut, but she was ugly. The next day, he saw near the residenz of Laeken, an Englishwoman with carroty-red hair and light-green shoes; but she was as thin, as a frog that has been shut up in a bottle for six months, to act as a barometer, which rendered her inapt to realize an ideal after the style of Rubens.

Finding that Brussels was peopled solely by Andalusians with burnished breasts – which fact is readily explained by the Spanish domination that held the Low Countries in subjection so long – Tiburce determined to go to Antwerp, thinking, with some appearance of reason, that the types familiar to Rubens and so constantly reproduced on his canvases were likely to be frequently met with in his beloved native city.

He betook himself, therefore, to the station of the railway that runs from Brussels to Antwerp. The steam horse had already eaten his ration of coal; he was snorting impatiently and blowing from his inflamed nostrils, with a strident noise, dense puffs of white smoke, mingled with showers of sparks. Tiburce seated himself in his compartment, in company with five Walloons, who sat as motionless in their places as canons in the chapter-house, and the train started. The pace was moderate at first; they moved little faster than one rides in a post chaise at ten francs the relay; but soon the beast became excited and was seized with a most extraordinary rage for rapidity. The poplars beside the track fled to right and left like a routed army; the landscape became blurred and was blotted out in a grey vapor; the colewort and the peony studded the black strips of ground with indistinct stars of gold and azure. Here and there a slender spire appeared amid the billowing clouds and disappeared instantly, like the mast of a ship on a stormy sea. Tiny light-pink or apple-green wine-shops made a fleeting impression on the eye at the rear of their gardens, beneath their garlands of vines or hops; here and there pools of water, encircled by dark mud, dazzled the eye like the mirror in a trap for larks. Meanwhile the iron monster belched forth with an ever-increasing roar its breath of boiling steam; it puffed like an asthmatic whale; a fiery sweat bathed its brazen sides. It seemed to complain of the insensate swiftness of its pace and to pray for mercy to its begrimed postillions, who spurred it on incessantly with shovelfuls of coal. There came a noise of bumping carriages and rattling chains: they had arrived.

Tiburce ran to right and left without fixed purpose, like a rabbit suddenly released from its cage. He took the first street that he saw, then a second, then a third, and plunged bravely into the heart of the ancient city, seeking the blonde with an ardor worthy of the knights-errant of old.

He saw a vast number of houses painted mouse-grey, canary-yellow, sea-green, pale lilac; with roofs like stairways, molded gables, doors with vermiculated bosses, with short stout pillars, decorated with quadrangular bracelets like those at the Luxembourg, leaded Renaissance windows, gargoyles, carved beams, and a thousand curious architectural details, which would have enchanted him on any other occasion; he barely glanced at the illuminated Madonnas, at the Christs bearing lanterns at the street corners, at the saints of wax or wood with their gewgaws and tinsel – all those Catholic emblems that have so strange a look to an inhabitant of one of our Voltairean cities. Another thought absorbed him: his eyes sought, through the dark, smoke-begrimed windows, some fair-haired feminine apparition, a tranquil and kindly

Brabantine face, with the ruddy freshness of the peach, and smiling within its halo of golden hair.

He saw only old women making lace, reading prayer-books, or squatting in corners and watching for the passing of an infrequent pedestrian, reflected by the glass of their espions, or by the ball of polished steel hanging in the doorway.

The streets were deserted, and more silent than those of Venice; no sound was to be heard save that of the chimes of various churches striking the hours in every possible key, for at least twenty minutes. The pavements, surrounded by a fringe of weeds, like those in the courtyards of unoccupied houses, told of the infrequency and small number of the passersby. Skimming the ground like stealthy swallows, a few women, wrapped discreetly in the folds of their dark hoods, glided noiselessly along the houses, sometimes followed by a small boy carrying their dog. Tiburce quickened his pace, in order to catch a glimpse of the features buried beneath the shadow of the hood, and saw there pale faces, with compressed lips, eyes surrounded by dark circles, prudent chins, delicate and circumspect noses – the genuine type of the pious Roman or the Spanish duenna; his burning glance was shattered against dead glances, the glassy stare of a dead fish.

From square to square, from street to street, Tiburce arrived at last at the Quay of the Scheldt by the Harbor Gate. The magnificent spectacle extorted a cry of surprise from him; an endless number of masts, yards, and cordage resembled a forest on the river, stripped of leaves and reduced to the state of a mere skeleton. The bowsprits and lateen yards rested familiarly on the parapet of the wharf, as a horse rests his head on the neck of his carriage-mate. There were Dutch orques, round-sterned, with their red sails; sharp, black American brigs, with cordage as fine as silk thread; salmon-colored Norwegian koffs, emitting a penetrating odor of planed fir; barges, fishermen, Breton salt-vessels, English coalers, ships from all parts of the world. An indescribable odor of sour herring, tobacco, rancid suet, melted tar, heightened by the acrid smells of the ships from Batavia, loaded with pepper, cinnamon, ginger and cochineal, floated about in the air in dense puffs, like the smoke from an enormous perfume-pan lighted in honor of commerce.

Tiburce, hoping to find the true Flemish type among the lower classes entered the taverns and gin-shops. He drank lambick, white beer of Louvain, ale, porter, and whisky, desiring to improve the opportunity to make the acquaintance of the northern Bacchus. He also smoked cigars of several brands, ate salmon, sauerkraut, yellow potatoes, rare roast-beef, and partook of all the delights of the country.

While he was dining, German women, chubby-faced, swarthy as gypsies, with short skirts and Alsatian caps, came to his table and squalled unmelodiously some dismal ballad, accompanying themselves on the violin and other un-pleasant instruments. Blonde Germany, as if to mock at Tiburce, had besmeared itself with the deepest shade of sunburn; he tossed them angrily a handful of small coins, which procured him the favor of another ballad of gratitude, shriller and more uncivilized than the first.

In the evening he went to the music halls to see the sailors dance with their mistresses; all of the latter had beautiful glossy black hair that shone like a crow's wing. A very pretty Creole seated herself beside him and familiarly touched her lips to his glass, according to the custom of the country, and tried to enter into conversation with him in excellent Spanish, for she was from Havana; she had such velvety-black eyes, a pale complexion, so warm and golden, such a small foot, and such a slender figure, that Tiburce, exasperated, sent her to all the devils, to the great surprise of the poor creature, who was little accustomed to such a greeting.

Utterly insensible to the dark perfections of the dancers, Tiburce with-drew to the Arms of Brabant Hotel. He undressed in a dissatisfied frame of mind, and wrapping himself as well as he could in the openwork napkins which take the place of sheets in Flanders, he soon slept the sleep of the just.

He had the loveliest dreams imaginable.

The nymphs and allegorical figures of the Medici Galley, in the most enticing déshabillé, paid him a nocturnal visit; they gazed fondly at him with their great blue eyes, and smiled at him in the most friendly way, with their lips blooming like red flowers amid the milky whiteness of their round, plump faces. One of them, the Nereid in the picture called The Queen's Voyage, carried familiarity so far as to pass her pretty taper fingers, tinged with carmine, through the hair of the lovelorn sleeper. Drapery of flowered brocade cleverly concealed the deformity of her scaly legs, ending in a forked tail; her fair hair was adorned with seaweed and coral, as befits a daughter of the sea; she was adorable in that guise. Groups of chubby children, as red as roses, swam about in a luminous atmosphere, holding aloft wreaths of flowers of insupportable brilliancy, and drew down from heaven a perfumed rain. At a sign from the Nereid, the nymphs stood in two rows and tied together the ends of their long auburn hair, in such wise as to form a sort of hammock of gold filigree for the fortunate Tiburce and his finny mistress; they took their places therein, and the nymphs swung them to and fro, moving their heads slightly with a rhythm of infinite sweetness.

Suddenly there was a sharp noise, the golden threads broke, and Tiburce fell to the ground. He opened his eyes and saw naught save a horrible bronze-colored face, which fastened upon him two great enamel eyes, only the whites of which could be seen.

"Your breakfast, mein Herr," said an old Hottentot negress, a servant of the hotel, placing on a small table a salver laden with dishes and silverware.

"Damnation! I ought to have gone to Africa to look for blondes!" grumbled Tiburce, as he attacked his beefsteak in desperation.

II
CHESTNUT HAIR

Tiburce, having duly satisfied his appetite, left the Arms of Brabant with the laudable and conscientious purpose of continuing the search for his ideal. He was no more fortunate than on the previous day; dark-skinned ironies, emerging from every street, cast sly and mocking glances at him; India, Africa, America, passed before him in specimens more or less copper-colored; one would have said that the venerable city, advised of his purpose, concealed in a spirit of mockery, in the depths of its most impenetrable back yards and behind its dingiest windows, all those of its daughters who might have recalled, vividly or remotely, the paintings of Jordaems or Rubens; stingy with its gold it was lavish with its ebony.

Enraged by this sort of mute ridicule, Tiburce visited the museums and galleries, to escape it. The Flemish Olympus shone once more before his eyes. Once more cascades of hair glistened in tiny reddish waves, with aquiver of gold and radiance; the shoulders of the allegories, refurbishing their silvery whiteness, glowed more vividly than ever; the blue of the eyes became lighter, the ruddy cheeks bloomed like bunches of carnations; a pink vapor infused warmth into the bluish pallor of the knees, elbows, and fingers of all those fair-haired goddesses; soft gleams of changing light, ruddy reflections, played over the plump, rounded flesh; the pigeon-breast draperies swelled before the breath of an invisible wind, and began to flutter about in the azure vapor; the fresh, plump Netherlandish poesy was revealed in all its entirety to our enthusiastic traveler.

But these beauties on canvas were not enough for him. He had come thither in search of real, living types. He had fed long enough on written and painted poetry, and he had discovered that intercourse with abstractions was somewhat unsubstantial. Doubtless it would have been much simpler to stay in Paris and fall in love with a pretty woman, or even with an ugly one, like everybody else; but Tiburce did not understand nature and was able to read it only in translations. He grasped admirably all the types realized in the works of the masters, but he would not have noticed them of his own motion if he had met them on the street or in society; in a word, if he had been a painter, he would have made vignettes based on the verses of poets; if he had been a poet, he would have written verses based on the pictures of painters. Art had taken possession of him when he was too young and had corrupted him and prejudiced him. Such instances are more common than is supposed in our overrefined civilization, where we come in contact with the works of man more often than with those of nature.

For a moment Tiburce had an idea of compromising with himself, and made this cowardly and ill-sounding remark: "Chestnut-hair is a very pretty color." He even went so far, the sycophant, the villain, the man of little faith, as to admit to himself that black eyes were very bright and very attractive. It may be said, to excuse him, that he had scoured in every direction, and without the slightest result, a city which everything justified him in believing to be radically blonde. A little discouragement was quite pardonable.

At the moment that he uttered this blasphemy under his breath, a lovely blue glance, wrapped in a mantilla, flashed before him and disappeared like a will-o'-the-wisp around the corner of Mei'r Square.

Tiburce quickened his pace, but he saw nothing more; the street was deserted from end to end. Evidently the flying vision had entered one of the neighboring houses, or had vanished in some unknown alley. Tiburce, bitterly disappointed, after glancing at the well, with the iron scrollwork forged by Quintin Metzys, the painter-locksmith, took it into his head to visit the cathedral, which he found daubed from top to bottom with a horrible canary-yellow. Luckily the wooden pulpit, carved by Verbruggen, with its decorations of foliage alive with birds, squirrels, and turkeys displaying their plumage, and all the zoological equipage which surrounded Adam and Eve in the terrestrial paradise, redeemed that general insipidity by the delicacy of its angles and its nicety of detail. Luckily, the blazonry of the noble families, and the pictures of Otto Venius, of Rubens, and of Van Dyck, partly concealed that hateful color, so dear to the middle classes and to the clergy.

A number of Beguins at prayer were scattered about on the pavement of the church; but the fervor of their piety caused them to bend their faces so low over their red-edged prayer-books, that it was difficult to distinguish their features. Moreover, the sanctity of the spot and the venerable aspect of their costumes prevented Tiburce from feeling inclined to carry his investigation farther.

Five or six Englishmen, breathless after ascending and descending the four hundred and seventy stairs of the steeple to which the dove's-nests with which it is always capped give the aspect of an Alpine peak, were examining the pictures and, trusting only in part to their guide's loquacious learning, were hunting up in their guidebooks the names of the masters, for fear of admiring one thing for another; and they repeated in front of every canvas, with imperturbable stolidity: "It is a very fine exhibition." These Englishmen had squarely-cut faces, and the enormous distance between their noses and their chins demonstrated the purity of the breed. As for the English lady who was with them, she was the same one whom Tiburce had previously seen at the residenz of Laeken; she wore the same green boots and the same red hair. Tiburce, despairing of finding Flemish blondes, was almost on the point of darting a killing glance at her; but the vaudeville couplets aimed at perfidious Albion came to his mind most opportunely.

In honor of these visitors, so manifestly Britannic, who could not move without a jingling of guineas, the beadle opened the shutters which, during three-fourths of the year, concealed the two wonderful paintings of the Crucifixion and the Descent from the Cross.

The Crucifixion is a work that stands by itself, and Rubens, when he painted it, was thinking of Michelangelo. The drawing is rough, savage, impetuous, like those of the Roman school; all the muscles stand out at once, all the bones and sinews are visible, nerves of steel are surrounded by flesh like granite. Here is no trace of the joyous, ruddy tones with which the Antwerpian artist nonchalantly sprinkles his innumerable productions; it is the Italian bistre in its tawniest intensity; executioners, colossi shaped like elephants, have tigers' muzzles and attitudes of bestial ferocity; even the Christ Himself, included in this exaggeration, wears rather the aspect of a Milo of Crotona, nailed to a wooden horse by rival athletes, than of a God voluntarily sacrificing Himself for the redemption of humanity. There is nothing Flemish in the picture save the great Snyders dog barking in a corner.

When the shutters of the Descent from the Cross were thrown open, Tiburce was dazzled and seized with vertigo as if he had looked into an abyss of blinding light; the sublime head of the Magdalen blazed triumphantly in an ocean of gold, and seemed to illuminate with the beams from its eyes the pale, grey atmosphere that filtered through the narrow Gothic windows. Everything about him faded away; there was an absolute void; the square-jawed Englishman, the red-haired English woman, the violet-robed beadle – he saw them no more.

The sight of that face was to Tiburce a revelation from on high; scales fell from his eyes, he found himself face to face with his secret dream, with his unavowed hope; the intangible image which he had pursued with all the ardor of an amorous imagination, and of which he had been able to espy only the profile or the ravishing fold of a dress; the capricious and untamed chimera, always ready to unfold its restless wings, was there before him, fleeing no more, motionless in the splendor of its beauty. The great master had copied in his own heart the anticipated and longed-for mistress; it seemed to him that he himself had painted the picture; the hand of genius had drawn unerringly and with broad strokes of the brush, what was only confusedly sketched in his mind, and had garbed in gorgeous colors his undefined fancy for the unknown. He recognized that race, and yet he had never seen it.

He stood there, mute, absorbed, as insensible as a man in a cataleptic fit, not moving an eyelid and plunging his eyes into the boundless glance of the great penitent.

A foot of the Christ, white with a bloodless whiteness, as pure and lifeless as a consecrated wafer, hovered with all the inert listlessness of death over the saint's white shoulder, an ivory footstool placed there by the sublime artist to enable the divine corpse to descend from the tree of redemption. Tiburce felt jealous of the Christ. For such a blessed privilege he would gladly have endured the Passion. The bluish pallor of the flesh hardly reassured him. He was deeply wounded, too, because the Magdalen did not turn towards him her melting, glistening eye, wherein the light bestowed its diamonds and grief its pearls. The dolorous and impassioned persistence of that glance, which wrapped the beloved body in a winding-sheet of love, seemed to him humiliating, and eminently unjust to him, Tiburce. He would have rejoiced if the most imperceptible gesture had given him to understand that she was touched by his love; he had already forgotten that he was standing before a painting, so quick is passion to attribute its own ardor even to objects incapable of feeling it. Pygmalion must have been astonished, as if it were a most extraordinary thing, that his statue did not return caress for caress; Tiburce was no less shocked by the coldness of his painted sweetheart.

Kneeling in her robe of green satin, with its ample and swelling folds, she continued to gaze upon the Christ with an expression of grief-stricken concupiscence, like a mistress who seeks to surfeit herself with the features of an adored face which she is never to see again; her hair fell over her shoulders, a luminous fringe; a sunbeam, straying in by chance, heightened the warm whiteness of her linen and of her arms of gilded marble; in the wavering light her breast seemed to swell and throb with an appearance of life; the tears in her eyes melted, and flowed like human tears.

Tiburce thought that she was about to rise and step down from the picture.

Suddenly there was darkness: the vision vanished.

The English visitors had withdrawn, after observing: "Very well; a pretty picture"; and the beadle, annoyed by Tiburce's prolonged contemplation, had closed the shutters, and was demanding the usual fee. Tiburce gave him all that he had in his pocket; lovers are generous to duennas; the Antwerpian beadle was the Magdalen's duenna, and Tiburce, already looking forward to another interview, was interested in obtaining his favorable consideration.

The colossal St. Christopher, and the hermit carrying a lantern, painted on the exterior of the shutters, albeit very remarkable works, were far from consoling Tiburce for the closing of that dazzling tabernacle, whence the genius of Rubens sparkles like a monstrance laden with precious stones.

He left the church, carrying in his heart the barbed arrow of an impossible love; he had at last fallen in with the passion that he sought, but he was punished where he had sinned: he had become too fond of painting, he was doomed to love a picture. Nature, neglected for art, revenged herself in barbarous fashion; the most timid lover in the presence of the most virtuous of women, always retains a secret hope in a corner of his heart; as for Tiburce, he was sure of his mistress's resistance and he was perfectly well aware that he would never be happy; so that his passion was a genuine passion, a wild, insensate passion, capable of anything; it was especially remarkable for its disinterestedness.

Do not make too merry over Tiburce's love; how many men do we see deeply enamored of women whom they have never seen except in a box at the theater, to whom – they have never spoken, and even the sound of whose voice they do not know! Are such men much more reasonable than our hero, and are their impalpable idols to be compared with the Magdalen at Antwerp?

Tiburce walked the streets with a proud and mysterious air, like a gallant returning from a first assignation. The intensity of his sensations surprised him agreeably – he who had never lived except in the brain felt the beating of his heart. It was a novel sensation; and so he abandoned himself without reserve to the charms of that unfamiliar impression; a real woman would not have touched him so deeply. An artificial man can be moved only by an artificial thing; there is a harmony between them; the true would create a discord. As we have said, Tiburce had read much, seen much, thought much, and felt very little; his fancies were simply brain fancies; in him passion rarely went below the cravat. But this time he was really in love, just like a student of rhetoric; the dazzling image of the Magdalen floated before his eyes in luminous spots, as if he had been looking at the sun; the slightest fold, the most imperceptible detail stood out clearly in his memory; the picture was always present before him. He tried in all seriousness to devise some means to impart life to that insensible beauty and to induce her to come forth from her frame; he thought of Prometheus, who kindled the fire of heaven in order to give a soul to his lifeless work; of Pygmalion, who succeeded in finding a way to move and warm a block of marble; he had an idea of plunging into the bottomless ocean of the occult sciences, in order to discover a charm sufficiently powerful to give life and substance to that vain appearance. He raved, he was mad: he was in love, you see.

Have you not yourself, without reaching that pitch of excitement, been invaded by a feeling of indescribable melancholy in a gallery of old masters, while thinking of the vanished beauties represented by their pictures? Would not one be glad to infuse life into all those pale and silent faces which seem to muse sadly against the greenish ultra-marine or the coal-black which forms the background? Those eyes, whose vital spark gleams more brightly beneath the veil of age, were copied from those of a young princess or a lovely courtesan, of whom naught remains, not even a single grain of dust; those lips, half parted in a painted smile, recall real smiles forever fled. What a pity, in truth, that the women of Raphael, of Correggio, and of Titian are but impalpable shades! And why have not the models, like their portraits, received the privilege of immortality? The harem of the most voluptuous sultan would be a small matter compared with that which one might form with the odalisques of painting, and it is really to be regretted that so much beauty is lost.

Tiburce went every day to the cathedral, and lost himself in contemplation of his beloved Magdalen; and he returned to the hotel each evening, more in love, more depressed, and more insane than ever. More than one noble heart, even without caring for pictures, has known the sufferings of our friend, when trying to breathe his soul into some lifeless idol, who had only the outward phantom of life, and realized the passion she inspired no more than a colored figure.

With the aid of powerful glasses our lover scrutinized his inamorata even in the most imperceptible details. He admired the fineness of the flesh, the solidity and suppleness of the coloring, the energy of the brush, the vigor of the drawings, as another would admire the velvety softness of the skin, the whiteness and the beautiful coloring of a living mistress. On the pretext of examining the work at closer range, he obtained a ladder from his friend, the beadle, and, all aquiver with love, he dared to rest a presumptuous hand on the Magdalen's shoulder. He was greatly surprised to feel, instead of the satinlike softness of a woman's flesh, a hard, rough surface like a file, with hollows and ridges everywhere, due to the impetuosity of the impulsive painter's brush. This discovery greatly depressed Tiburce, but, as soon as he had descended to the floor again, his illusion returned.

He passed more than a fortnight thus, in a state of transcendental enthusiasm, wildly stretching out his arms to his chimera, imploring Heaven to perform a miracle. In his lucid moments he resigned himself to the alternative of seeking throughout the city some type approaching his ideal; but his search resulted in nothing, for one does not find readily on streets and public promenades such a diamond of beauty.

One evening, however, he met again, at the corner of Mei'r Square, the charming blue glance we have previously mentioned; this time the vision disappeared less quickly, and Tiburce had time to see a lovely face framed by rich clusters of fair hair, and an artless smile playing about the freshest lips in the world. She quickened her pace when she realized that she was followed, but Tiburce, keeping at a distance, saw her stop in front of a respectable old Flemish house, of poor but decent aspect. As there was some delay in admitting her, she turned for an instant, doubtless in obedience to a vague instinct of feminine coquetry, to see if the stranger had been discouraged by the long walk she had compelled him to take. Tiburce as if enlightened by a sudden gleam of light, saw that she bore a striking resemblance to – the Magdalen.

III
RESEMBLANCE

The house which the slender figure had entered had an air of Flemish simplicity altogether patriarchal. It was painted a faded rose-color, with narrow white lines to represent the joints of the stones. The gable, denticulated like the steps of a staircase; the roof with its round windows surrounded by scrollwork; the impost, representing, with Gothic artlessness, the story of Noah derided by his sons; the stork's nest, and the pigeons making their toilet in the sun, made it a perfect example of its type; you would have said that it was one of those factories so common in the pictures of Van der Heyden and of Teniers.

A few stalks of hops softened with their playful greenery the too severe and too methodical aspect of the house as a whole. The lower windows were provided with round bars, and over the two lower panes were squares of muslin embroidered with great bunches of flowers after the Brussels fashion; in the space left empty by the swelling of the iron bars were china pots containing a few pale carnations of sickly aspect, despite the evident care the owner took of them, for their drooping heads were supported by playing-cards and a complicated system of tiny scaffolding of twigs of osier. Tiburce observed this detail, which indicated a chaste and restrained life, a whole poem of youth and beauty.

As, after two hours of waiting, he had not seen the fair Magdalen with the blue eyes come forth, he sagely concluded that she must live there; which was true. All that he had left to do was to learn her name, her position in society, to become acquainted with her, and to win her love; mere trifles, in very truth. A professional Lovelace would not have been delayed five minutes; but honest Tiburce was not a Lovelace; on the contrary, he was bold in thought, but timid in action; no one was less clever than he at passing from the general to the particular, and in love affairs he had a most pressing need of a truthworthy Pandarus to extol his perfections and to arrange his rendezvous. Once under way, he did not lack eloquence; he declaimed the languorous harangue with due self-possession, and played the lover at least as well as a provincial jeune premier; but, unlike Petit-Jean, the clog's lawyer, the part that he was least expert at was the beginning.

We are bound to admit, therefore, that worthy Tiburce swam in a sea of uncertainty, devising a thousand stratagems more ingenious than those of Polybius, to gain access to his divinity. As he found nothing suitable, he conceived the idea, like Don Cleofas in the Diable Boiteux, of setting fire to the house, in order to have an opportunity to rescue his darling from the flames and thus to prove to her his courage and his devotion; but he reflected that a fireman, more accustomed than he to roam about on burning rafters, might supplant him; and, moreover, that the method of making a pretty girl's acquaintance was forbidden by the Code.

Awaiting a better inspiration, he engraved very clearly on his brain the location of the house, noted the name of the street, and returned to his hotel, reasonably content, for he had imagined that he saw vaguely outlined behind the embroidered muslin at the window the graceful silhouette of the unknown, and a tiny hand put aside a corner of the transparent fabric, doubtless to make sure of his virtuous persistence in standing sentry, without hope of being relieved, at the corner of a lonely street in Antwerp. Was this mere conceit on the part of Tiburce, and was his bonne fortune one of those common to nearsighted men, who mistake linen hanging in the window for the scarf of Juliet leaning over toward Romeo, and pots of flowers for princesses in gowns of gold brocade? However that may have been, he went away in high spirits, looking upon himself as one of the most triumphant of gallants. The hostess of the Arms of Brabant and her black maidservant were surprised at the airs of Hamilcar and of a drum-major which he assumed. He lighted his cigar in the most determined fashion, crossed his legs, and began to dandle his slipper on his toes with the superb nonchalance of a mortal who utterly despises all creation, and who is blessed with joys unknown to the ordinary run of mankind; he had at last found the blonde. Jason was no happier when he took the marvelous token from the enchanted tree.

Our hero was in the best of all possible situations: a genuine Havana cigar in his mouth, slippers on his feet, a bottle of Rhine wine on his table, with the newspapers of the past week and a pretty little pirated edition of the poems of Alfred de Musset.

He could drink a glass, or even two, of Tokay, read Namouna, or an account of the latest ballet; there is no reason, therefore, why we should not leave him alone for a few moments; we have given him enough to dispel his ennui, assuming that a lover can ever suffer from ennui. We will return without him – for he is not the sort of a man to open the doors for us – to the little house on Rue Kipdorp, and we will act as introducers, we will show you what there is behind the embroidered muslin of the lower windows; for, as our first piece of information, we will tell you that the heroine of this tale lived on the ground floor and her name was Gretchen; a name which, albeit not so euphonious as Ethelwina, or Azalia, seemed sufficiently sweet to German or Dutch ears.

Enter, after carefully wiping your feet, for Flemish cleanliness reigns despotically here. In Flanders, people wash their faces only once a week, but by way of compensation the floors are scalded and scraped to the quick twice a day. The floor in the hall, like those in the rest of the house, is made of pine boards, whose natural color is retained, the long, pale veins and the starlike knots being hidden by no varnish; it is sprinkled with a light coating of sea-sand, carefully sifted, the grains of which hold the feet and prevent the slipping so frequent in our salons, where one skates rather than walks. Gretchen's bedroom is at the right, behind that door painted a modest grey, whose copper knob, scoured with pumice, shines as if it were of gold; rub your feet once more upon this mat of rushes; the emperor himself might not enter with muddy feet.

Observe an instant this placid and peaceful interior; there is nothing to attract the eye; everything is calm, sober, restrained; the chamber of Marguerite herself produces no more virginal impression; it is the serenity of innocence which presides over all these petty details so fascinatingly neat.

The brown walls, with an oaken wainscoting waist-high, have no other ornament than a Madonna in colored plaster, dressed in real fabrics like a doll, with satin shoes, a wreath of rushes, a necklace of colored glass, and two small vases of artificial flowers in front of her. At the rear of the room, in the corner most in the shadow, stands a four-posted bed of antique shape, with curtains of green serge and valances with pinked edges and a hem of yellow lace. By the pillow, a figure of the Christ, the lower part of the cross forming a holy water vessel, stretches His ivory arms above the chaste maiden's slumbers.

A chest which glistens like a mirror, so diligently is it rubbed; a table with twisted legs standing near the window, and covered with spools, skeins of silk, and all the paraphernalia of lacework; a huge, upholstered easy chair, three or four high-backed, chairs of the style of Louis XIII, such as we see in the engravings of Abraham Bosse, composed the furnishing, almost puritanical in its simplicity.

We must add, however, that Gretchen, innocent as she was, had indulged in the luxury of a Venetian mirror, with beveled edges, surrounded by a frame of ebony encrusted with copper. To be sure, to sanctify that profane object, a twig of blessed boxwood was stuck in the frame.

Imagine Gretchen sitting in the great upholstered easy chair, with her feet upon a stool embroidered by herself, entangling and disentangling with her fairy fingers the almost imperceptible network of a piece of lace just begun; her pretty head leaning over her work is lighted from below by a thousand frolicsome reflections which brighten with fresh and vapory tints the transparent shadow in which she is bathed; a delicate bloom of youth softens the somewhat too Dutch ruddiness of her cheeks, whose freshness the half-light cannot impair; the daylight, admitted sparingly through the upper panes, touches only the top of her brow, and makes the little wisps of hair that rebel against the restraint of the comb gleam like golden tendrils. Cause a sudden ray of sunlight to play upon the cornice and upon the chest, sprinkle dots of gold over the rounded sides of the pewter pots, make the Christ a little yellower; retouch with a deeper shadow the stiff, straight folds of the serge curtains; darken the modernized pallor of the window-glass; stand old Barbara, armed with her broom, at the end of the room, concentrate all the light upon the maiden's head and hands, and you will have a Flemish painting of the best period, which Terburg or Gaspard Netscher would not refuse to sign.

What a contrast between that interior, so clean and neat and so easily understood, and the bedroom of a young Frenchwoman, always filled with clothes, with music-paper, with unfinished watercolors; where every article is out of its place; where tumbled dresses hang on the backs of chairs; and where the household cat tears with her claws the novel carelessly left on the floor! How clear and crystalline is the water in which that half-withered rose stands! How white that linen, how clear and transparent that glassware! Not a particle of dust in the air, not a rug out of place.

Metzu, who painted in a summer-house situated in the center of a lake, in order to preserve the integrity of his colors, might have worked without annoyance in Gretchen's bedroom. The iron back of the fire-place shines like a silver bas-relief.

At this point a sudden apprehension seizes us; is she really the heroine suited to our hero? Is Gretchen really Tiburce's ideal? Is not all this very minute, very commonplace, very practical? is it not rather the Dutch than the Flemish type, and do you really believe that Ruben's models were built like her? Was it not rather merry gossips, highly-colored, abounding in flesh, of robust health, and careless and vulgar manners, whose commonplace reality the painter's genius has idealized? The great masters often play us such tricks. Of an indifferent site they make a lovely landscape; of an ugly maidservant, a Venus; they do not copy what they see, but what they desire.

And yet Gretchen, although daintier and more refined, really bore a striking resemblance to the Magdalen of Antwerp Cathedral, and Tiburce's imagination might well rest upon her without going astray. It would have been hard for him to find a more magnificent body for the phantom of his painted mistress. You desire, doubtless, now that you know Gretchen and her bedroom, the bird and its nest, as well as we ourselves do, to have some details concerning her life and her social position. Her history was as simple as possible: Gretchen was the daughter of small trades-people who had been unfortunate, and she had been an orphan for several years; she lived with Barbara, a devoted old servant, upon a small income, the remains of her father's property, and upon the proceeds of her work; as Gretchen made her own dresses and her laces, as she was looked upon by the Flemings as a prodigy of prudence and neatness, she was able, although a simple working-girl, to dress with a certain elegance, and to differ little from the daughters of citizens of the middle class; her linen was fine, her caps were always notable for their whiteness; her boots were the best made in the city; for – we trust that this detail will not displease Tiburce – we must admit that Gretchen had the foot of a Spanish countess, and shod herself to correspond. She was a well-educated girl; she knew how to read, could write well, knew all possible stitches in embroidery, had no rival on earth in needlework, and did not play the piano. Let us add that she had by way of compensation an admirable talent for cooking pear-tarts, carp au bleu, and cake; for she prided herself on her culinary skill, like all good housekeepers, and knew how to prepare a thousand little delicacies after her own recipes.

These details will seem without doubt far from aristocratic, but our heroine is neither a princess of diplomacy nor a charming woman of thirty, nor a fashionable singer; she is a simple working-girl of Rue Kipdorp, near the ramparts, Antwerp; but as, in our eyes, women have no real distinction save their beauty, Gretchen is the equal of a duchess who is entitled to sit in the king's presence, and we look upon her sixteen years as sixteen quarterings of nobility.

What was the state of Gretchen's heart? The state of her heart was most satisfactory; she had never loved anything but coffee-colored turtle-doves, gold-fish, and other absolutely innocent small creatures, which could not cause the most savagely jealous lover a moment's anxiety. Every Sunday she went to hear high mass at the Jesuits' church, modestly wrapped in her hood and attended by Barbara carrying her book; then she went home and turned over the leaves of a Bible, "in which God the Father was represented in the costume of an emperor," and of which the wood-engravings aroused her admiration for the thousandth time. If the weather was fine, she went out to Lillo fort, or to the Head of Flanders, with a girl of her own age, also a lace-worker. During the week she seldom went out, except to deliver her work; and Barbara undertook that duty most of the time. A girl of sixteen years who has never thought of love would be an improbable character in a warmer climate; but the atmosphere of Flanders, made heavy by the sickly exhalations from the canals, contains very few aphrodisiac molecules; the flowers are backward there, and when they come are thick and pulpy; their odors, laden with moisture, resemble the odors of decoctions of aromatic herbs; the fruits are watery; the earth and the sky, saturated with moisture, send back and forth the vapors which they cannot absorb, and which the sun tries in vain to drink with its pale lips; the women who live in this bath of mist have no difficulty in being virtuous, for, according to Byron, that rascal of a sun is a great seducer and has made more conquests than Don Juan.

It is not surprising, therefore, that Gretchen, in such a moral atmosphere, was a perfect stranger to all ideas of love, even under the form of marriage, a legal and permissible form if such there be. She has read no bad novels, nor even any good ones; she had not any male relatives, cousins or second cousins. Lucky Tiburce! Moreover, the sailors with their short, colored pipes, the captains of the East-Indiamen who strolled about the city during their brief time on shore, and the dignified merchants who went to the Bourse, revolving figures in the wrinkles of their foreheads, and who cast their fleeting shadows into Gretchen's sanctum as they walked by the house, were not at all calculated to inflame the imagination.

Let us admit, however, that, despite her maidenly ignorance, the laceworker had remarked Tiburce as a well-turned cavalier with regular features; she had seen him several times at the cathedral, in rapt contemplation before the Descent from the Cross, and attributed his ecstatic attitude to an excessive piety most edifying in so young a man. As she whirled her bobbins about, she thought of the stranger of Mei'r Square, and abandoned herself to innocent reverie. One day even, under the influence of that thought, she rose, and unconscious of her own act, went to her mirror, which she consulted for a long while; she looked at herself full-faced, in profile, in all possible lights, and discovered – what was quite true – that her complexion was more silky than a sheet of rice or camellia paper; that she had blue eyes of a marvelous limpidity, charming teeth in a mouth as red as a peach, and fail hair of the loveliest shade. She noticed for the first time her youthful charm and her beauty; she took the white rose which stood in the pretty glass, placed it in her hair, and smiled to see how that simple flower embellished her; coquetry was born and love would soon follow it.

But it is a long time since we left Tiburce; what had he been doing at the Arms of Brabant, while we furnished this information concerning the lace-worker? He had written upon a very fine sheet of paper what was probably a declaration of love, unless it was a challenge; for several other sheets, besmeared and marred by erasures, which lay on the floor, proved that it was a document very difficult to draw up, and of great importance. After finishing it, he took his cloak and bent his steps once more toward Rue Kipdorp.

Gretchen's lamp, a star of peace and toil, shone softly behind the glass, and the shadow of the girl as she leaned over her work was cast upon the transparent muslin. Tiburce, more excited than a robber about to turn the key of a treasure-chest, drew near the window with the step of a wolf, passed his hand through the bars, and buried in the soft earth of the vase of carnations the corner of his letter thrice folded, hoping that Gretchen could not fail to see it when she opened her window in the morning to water her flowers. That done, he withdrew with a step as light as if the soles of his boots were covered with felt.

IV
A CERTIFICATE OF BEAUTY

The fresh blue light of the morning paled the sickly yellow of the lanterns, which were almost burned out; the Scheldt streamed like a sweating horse, and the daylight was beginning to filter through the rents in the mist, when Gretchen's window opened. Gretchen's eyes were still swimming in languor, and the mark left on her delicate cheek by a fold of the pillow showed that she had slept without moving in her little virginal bed, that profound sleep of which youth alone has the secret. She was anxious to see how her dear carnations had passed the night, and had hastily wrapped herself in the first garment that came to hand; that graceful and modest déshabillé became her wondrously; and if the idea of a goddess can be reconciled with a little cap of Flanders, linen embellished with lace, and a dressing-sack of white dimity, we will venture to say that she had the aspect of Aurora opening the gates of the East; this comparison is perhaps a little too majestic for a laceworker who is about to water a garden contained in two porcelain pots; but surely Aurora was less fresh and rosy, especially the Aurora of Flanders, whose eyes are always a little dull.

Gretchen, armed with a large pitcher, prepared to water her carnations, and Tiburce's ardent declaration came very near being drowned beneath a moral deluge of cold water; luckily the white paper caught Gretchen's eye; she disinterred the letter and was greatly surprised when she saw the contents. There were only two sentences, one in French, the other in German; the French sentence was composed of two words, "je t'aime;" the German of three, "ich liebe dich;" which means exactly the same thing – "I love you." Tiburce had provided for the possibility that Gretchen would understand only her mother tongue; he was, as you see, a consummately prudent person.

Really, it was well worth while to besmear more paper than Malherbe ever used to compose a stanza, and to drink, on the pretext of exciting the imagination, a bottle of excellent Tokay, in order to arrive at that ingenious and novel thought. But, despite its apparent simplicity, Tiburce's letter was perhaps a masterpiece of libertinism, unless it was mere folly, which is possible. However, was it not a master-stroke to let fall thus, like a drop of melted lead, into the midst of that tranquility of mind that single phrase, "I love you?" And was not its fall certain to produce, as on the surface of a lake, an infinite number of radiations and concentric circles?

In truth, what do all the most ardent love-letters contain? What remains of all the bombast of passion when one pricks it with the pin of reason? All the eloquence of Saint-Preux reduces itself to a phrase; and Tiburce had really attained great profundity by concentrating in that brief sentence the flowery rhetoric of his first drafts.

He did not sign it; indeed, what information would his name have given? He was a stranger in the city, he did not know Gretchen's name, and, to tell the truth, cared very little about it. The affair was more romantic, more mysterious thus; the least fertile imagination might build thereupon twenty octavo volumes more or less probable. Was he a sylph, a pure spirit, a lovelorn angel, a handsome officer, a banker's son, a young nobleman, a peer of England with an income of a million, a Russian feudal lord, with a name ending in off, many rubles, and a multitude of fur collars? Such were the serious questions which that laconically eloquent letter must inevitably raise. The familiar form of address, which is used only to Divinity, betrayed a violence of passion which Tiburce was very far from feeling, but which might produce the best effect upon the girl's mind, as exaggeration always seems more natural to a woman than the truth.

Gretchen did not hesitate an instant to believe the young man of Mei'r Square to be the author of the note; women never err in such matters; they have a wonderful instinct, a scent, which takes the place of familiarity with the world and knowledge of the passions. The most virtuous of them knows more than Don Juan with his list.

We have described our heroine as a very artless, very ignorant, and very respectable young woman; we must confess, however, that she did not feel the virtuous indignation which a woman ought to feel who receives a note written in two languages and containing such a decided incongruity. She felt rather a thrill of pleasure, and a faint pink flush passed over her face. That letter was to her like a certificate of beauty; it reassured her concerning herself, and gave her a definite rank; it was the first glance that had ever penetrated her modest obscurity; the small proportions of her fortune prevented her being sought in marriage. Thus far she had been considered simply as a child, Tiburce consecrated her a young woman; she felt for him such gratitude as the pearl must feel for the diver who discovers it in its coarse shell beneath the dark cloak of the ocean.

This first impression passed, Gretchen experienced a sensation well known to all those who have been brought up strictly, and who never have had a secret; the letter embarrassed her like a block of marble; she did not know what to do with it. Her room seemed to her not to have enough dark corners, enough impenetrable hiding places, in which to conceal it from all eyes. She put it in the chest behind a pile of linen; but after a few moments she took it out again; the letter blazed through the boards of the wardrobe like Doctor Faust's microcosm in Rembrandt's etching. Gretchen looked for another, safer place; Barbara might need napkins or sheets and might find it. She took a chair, stood upon it, and placed the letter on the canopy of her bed; the paper burned her hands like a piece of red-hot iron.

Barbara entered to arrange the room. Gretchen, affecting the most indifferent air imaginable, took her usual seat and resumed her work of the day before; but at every step that Barbara took toward the bed, she fell into a horrible fright; the arteries in her temples throbbed, the sweat of anguish stood upon her forehead, her fingers became entangled in the threads, and it seemed to her that an invisible hand was grasping her heart. Barbara seemed to her to have an uneasy, suspicious expression which was not customary with her. At last the old woman went out, with a basket on her arm, to do her marketing. Poor Gretchen breathed freely again, and took down her letter, which she put in her pocket; but soon it made her itch; the creaking of the paper terrified her, and she put it in her breast; for that is where a woman puts everything that embarrasses her. The waist of a dress is a cupboard without a key, an arsenal filled with flowers, locks of hair, lockets, and sentimental epistles; a sort of letter box, in which one mails all the correspondence of the heart.

But why did Gretchen not burn that insignificant scrap of paper which caused her such keen terror? In the first place, Gretchen had never in her life experienced such poignant emotion; she was terrified and enchanted at once. And then, pray tell us why lovers persist in not destroying letters which may lead later to their detection and perdition? It is because a letter is a visible soul; because passion has passed through that paltry sheet with its electric fluid, and has imparted life to it. To burn a letter is to commit a moral murder; in the ashes of a destroyed correspondence there are always some particles of two hearts.

So Gretchen kept her letter in the folds of her dress, beside a little gold crucifix, which was greatly surprised to find itself in close proximity to a love-letter.

Like a shrewd young man, Tiburce left his declaration time to work. He played the dead man and did not again appear in Rue Kipdorp. Gretchen was beginning to be alarmed, when one fine morning she perceived in the bars of her window a superb bouquet of exotic flowers. Tiburce had passed that way; that was his visiting-card.

The bouquet afforded much pleasure to the young working-girl, who had become accustomed to the thought of Tiburce, and whose self-esteem was secretly hurt by the small amount of zeal which he had shown after such an ardent beginning; she took the bunch of flowers, filled with water one of her pretty Saxon vases with a raised blue design, untied the stalks and put them in water, in order to keep them longer. On this occasion she told the first lie of her life, informing Barbara that the bouquet was a present from a lady to whom she had carried some lace, and who knew her liking for flowers.

During the day Tiburce came to cool his heels in front of the house, on the pretext of making a drawing of some odd bit of architecture; he remained for a long while, working with a blunt pencil on a piece of wretched vellum. Gretchen played the dead in her turn; not a fold stirred, not a window opened; the house seemed asleep. Entrenched in a corner, she was able by means of the mirror in her work-box to watch Tiburce at her ease. She saw that he was tall, well-built, with an air of distinction in his whole person, regular features, a soft and melting eye, and a melancholy expression, which touched her deeply, accustomed as she was to the rubicund health of Brabantine faces. Moreover, Tiburce, although he was neither a lion nor a dandy, did not lack natural refinement, and must have appeared an ultra-fashionable to a young girl so innocent as Gretchen; on Boulevard de Gand he would have seemed hardly up-to-date, on Rue Kipdorp he was magnificent.

In the middle of the night, Gretchen, obeying an adorable childish impulse, rose and went barefooted to look at her bouquet; she buried her face in the flowers, and kissed Tiburce on the red lips of a magnificent dahlia; she thrust her head passionately into the multicolored waves of that bath of flowers, inhaling with long breaths intoxicating perfume, breathing with full nostrils, until she felt her heart melt and her eyes grow moist. When she stood erect, her cheeks glistened with pearly drops, and her fascinating little nose, smeared as prettily as possible with the golden dust from the stamens, was a lovely shade of yellow. She wiped it laughingly, returned to bed and to sleep; as you may imagine, she saw Tiburce in all her dreams.

In all this what had become of the Magdalen of the Descent from the Cross? She still reigned without a rival in our young enthusiast's heart; she had the advantage over the loveliest living woman of being impossible; with her there was no disillusionment, no satiety; she did not break the spell by commonplace or absurd phrases; she was always there, motionless, adhering religiously to the sovereign lines within which the great master had confined her; sure of being beautiful to all eternity; and relating to the world in her silent language the dream of a sublime genius.

The little laceworker of Rue Kipdorp was truly a charming creature; but how far were her arms from having that undulating and supple contour, that potent energy, all enveloped with grace! how juvenile was the slender curve of her shoulders! and how pale the shade of her hair beside those strange, rich tones with which Rubens had warmed the rippling locks of the placid sinner! Such was the language which Tiburce used to himself as he walked upon the Quay of the Scheldt.

However, seeing that he made little progress in his love affair with the painting, he reasoned with himself most sensibly concerning his monumental folly. He returned to Gretchen, not without a long-drawn sigh of regret; he did not love her, but at all events she reminded him of his dream, as a daughter reminds one of an adored mother who is dead. We will not dwell on the details of this little intrigue, for everyone can easily imagine them. Chance, that great procurer, afforded our two lovers a very natural opportunity to speak.

Gretchen had gone as usual to the Head of Flanders on the other side of the Scheldt with her young friend. They had run after butterflies, made wreaths of blue-bottles, and rolled about on the straw in the mills, so long that night had come and the ferryman had made his last trip, unperceived by them. They were standing there, both decidedly perturbed, with one foot in the water, shouting with all the strength of their little silvery voices for him to come back and get them; but the playful breeze carried their shouts away, and there was no reply save the soft splashing of the waves on the sand. Luckily, Tiburce was drifting about in a small sailboat; he heard them and offered to take them across; an offer which the friend eagerly accepted, despite Gretchen's embarrassed air and her flushed cheeks. Tiburce escorted her home and took care to organize a boating party for the following Sunday, with the assent of Barbara, whom his assiduous attendance at the churches and his devotion to the picture of the Descent from the Cross had very favorably disposed.

Tiburce met with no great resistance on Gretchen's part. She was so pure that she did not defend herself, because she did not know that she was attacked; and besides, she loved Tiburce; for although he talked very jocosely and expressed himself upon all subjects with ironical heedlessness, she divined that he was unhappy, and a woman's instinct is to console: grief attracts them as a mirror attracts the lark.

Although the young Frenchman was most attentive to her and treated her with extreme courtesy, she felt that she did not possess his heart entirely, and that there were corners in his mind to which she never penetrated. Some hidden thought of superior moment seemed to engross him and it was evident that he made frequent journeys into an unknown world; his fancy, borne away by the involuntary flappings of its wings, lost its footing constantly and beat against the ceiling, seeking, like a captive bird, some issue through which to dart forth into the blue sky. Often, he scrutinized her with extraordinary earnestness for hours at a time, sometimes with a satisfied expression, and again with an air of dissatisfaction. That look was not the look of a lover. Gretchen could not understand such behavior, but as she was sure of Tiburce's loyalty, she was not alarmed.

Tiburce, on the pretext that Gretchen's name was hard to pronounce, had christened her Magdalen, a substitution which she had gladly accepted, feeling a secret pleasure in having her lover call her by a different and mysterious name, as if she were to him another woman. He still made frequent visits to the cathedral, teasing his mania by impotent contemplations; and on those days Gretchen paid the penalty for the harsh treatment of the Magdalen; the real had to pay for the ideal. He was cross, bored, tiresome, which the honest creature ascribed to irritated nerves or too persistent reading.

Nevertheless, Gretchen was a charming girl, who deserved to be loved on her own account. Not in all the divisions of Flanders, in Brabant or Hainault, could you find a whiter and fresher skin and hair of a lovelier shade; her hand was at once plump and slender, with nails like agate, — a genuine princess's hand; and — a rare perfection in the country of Rubens — a small foot.

Ah! Tiburce, Tiburce, who longed to hold in your arms a real ideal, and to kiss your chimera on the mouth, beware! Chimeras, despite their rounded throats, their swan's wings, and then sparkling smiles, have sharp teeth and tearing claws. The evil creatures will pump the pure blood from your heart, and leave you dryer and more hollow than a sponge; avoid that unbridled ambition, do not try to make marble statues descend from their pedestals, and do not address your supplications to dumb canvases; all your painters and your poets were afflicted with the same disease that you have; they tried to make creations of their own in the midst of God's creation. With marble, with colors, with the rhythm of verses, they translated and defined their dream of beauty; their works are not the portraits of their mistresses, but of the mistresses they longed for and you would seek in vain their models on earth. Go and buy another bouquet for Gretchen, who is a sweet and lovely maiden; drop your dead women and your phantoms, and try to live with the people of this world.

V
TO PARIS!

Yes, Tiburce, though it will surprise you greatly to learn it, Gretchen is vastly superior to you. She has never read the poets, and does not even know the names of Homer and Virgil; the lamentations of the Wandering Jew, of Henriette and Damon, printed on wood and roughly-colored, compose all of her literature, except the Latin in her mass-book, which she spells out conscientiously every Sunday; Virginie knew little more in the solitude of her paradise of magnolias and roses.

You are, it is true, thoroughly posted in literary affairs. You are profoundly versed in esthetics, esoterics, plastics, architectonics, and poetics; Marphurius and Pancratius had not a finer list of acquirements in ics. From Orpheus and Lycophron down to M. de Lamartine's last volume, you have devoured everything that is composed of meters, of rimed lines, and of strophes cast in every possible mold; no romance has escaped you. You have traversed from end to end the vast world of the imagination; you know all the painters from Andrea Rico of Crete, and Bizzamano, down to Messieurs Ingres and Delacroix; you have studied beauty at its purest sources; the bas-reliefs of the friezes of the Parthenon, the Etruscan vases, the hieratic sculptures of Egypt, Greek art and Roman art, the Gothic and the Renaissance; you have searched and analyzed everything; you have become a sort of jockey of Beauty, whose advice painters take when they desire to select a model, as one consults a groom concerning the purchase of a horse. Certainly no one is more familiar than you with the physical side of woman; you are as expert as an Athenian sculptor on that point; but poetry has engrossed you so much that you have suppressed nature, the world, and life. Your mistresses have been to you simply pictures more or less satisfying; your love for the beauty and attractive ones was in the proportion of a Titian to a Coucher or a Vanloo; but you have never wondered whether anything real throbbed and vibrated beneath that exterior. Although you have a kind heart, grief and joy seem to you like two grimaces which disturb the tranquility of the outlines; woman is in your eyes a warm statue.

Ah! unhappy child, throw your books into the fire, tear your engraving, shatter your plaster casts, forget Raphael, forget Homer, forget Phidias, since you have not the courage to take a pencil, a pen, or a modeling-tool; of what use is this sterile admiration to you? what will be the end of these insane impulses? Do you demand more of life than it can give you? Great geniuses alone are entitled not to be content with creation. They can go and look the Sphinx squarely in the face, for they solve its riddles. But you are not a great genius; be simple of heart, love those who love you, and, as Jean Paul says, do not ask for moonlight, or for a gondola on Lake Mag'giore, or for a rendezvous at Isola Bella.

Become a philanthropic advocate or a concierge; limit your ambition to becoming a voter and a corporal in your company; have what in the world is called a trade; become an honest citizen. At these words no doubt your long hair will stand erect in horror, for you have the same scorn for the simple bourgeois that the German student professes for the Philistine, the soldier for the civilian, and the Brahma for the Pariah. You crush with ineffable disdain every worthy tradesman who prefers a vaudeville song to a tercet of Dante, and the muslin of fashionable portrait-painters to a sketch by Michelangelo. Such a man is in your eyes below the brute, and yet there are plain citizens whose minds – and they have minds – are rich with poetic feeling, who are capable of love and devotion, and who experience emotions of which you are incapable, yet whose brain has annihilated the heart.

Look at Gretchen, who has done nothing but water carnations and make lace all her life; she is a thousand times more poetic than you, monsieur l'artiste, as they say nowadays; she believes, she hopes, she smiles, and weeps; a word from you brings sunshine or rain to her lovely face; she sits there in her great upholstered armchair, beside her window, in a melancholy light, at work upon her usual task; but how her young brain labors! how fast her imagination travels! how many castles in Spain she builds and throws down! See her blush and turn pale, turn hot and cold, like the amorous maiden of the ancient ode; her lace drops from her hands, she has heard on the brick sidewalk a step which she distinguishes among a thousand, with all the acuteness which passion gives to the senses; although you arrive at the appointed time, she has been waiting for you a long while. All day you have been her sole preoccupation; she has asked herself: "Where is he now? – What is he doing? – Is he thinking of me as I am thinking of him? – Perhaps he is ill; yesterday he seemed to me paler than usual, and he had a distressed and preoccupied expression when he left me; can anything have happened to him? Has he received unpleasant news from Paris?" – and all those questions which love propounds to itself in its sublime disquietude.

That poor child, with her great loving heart, has displaced the center of her existence, she no longer lives except in you and through you. By virtue of the wonderful mystery of the incarnation of love, her soul inhabits your body, her spirit descends upon you and visits you; she would throw herself in front of the sword which should threaten your breast; the blow that should reach you would cause her death; and yet you have taken her up simply as a plaything, to use her as a manikin for your ideal. To merit such a wealth of love, you have darted a few glances at her, given her a few bouquets, and declaimed in a passionate tone the commonplaces of romance. A more earnest lover would have failed perhaps; for, alas! to inspire love, it is not necessary to feel it oneself. You have deliberately disturbed for all time the limpidity of that modest existence. Upon my word, Master Tiburce, adorer of the blonde type and contemner of the bourgeois, you have done a cruel thing; we regret to be obliged to tell you so.

Gretchen was not happy; she divined an invisible rival between herself and her lover and jealousy seized her; she watched Tiburce's movements, and saw that he went only to his hotel, the Arms of Brabant, and to the cathedral on Mei'r Square. She was reassured.

"What is the matter with you," she asked him once, "that you are always looking at the figure of the Magdalen supporting the Savior's body in the picture of the Descent from the Cross?"

"Because she looks like you," Tiburce replied.

Gretchen blushed with pleasure and ran to the mirror to verify the accuracy of the comparison; she saw that she had the unctuous and glowing eyes, the fair hair, the arched forehead, the general shape of the saint's face.

"So that is the reason that you call me Magdalen and not Gretchen, or Marguerite, which is my real name?"

"Precisely so," replied Tiburce, with an embarrassed air.

"I would never have believed that I was so lovely," said Gretchen; "and it makes me very happy, for you will love me better for it."

Serenity returned for some time to the maiden's heart, and we must confess that Tiburce made virtuous efforts to combat his insane passion. The fear of becoming a monomaniac came to his mind; and to cut short that obsession he determined to return to Paris.

Before starting, he went to pay one last visit to the cathedral, and his friend the beadle opened the shutters of the Descent from the Cross for him.

The Magdalen seemed to him more sad and disconsolate than usual; great tears rolled down her pallid cheeks, her mouth was contracted by a spasm of grief, a bluish circle surrounded her melting eyes, the sunbeam had left her hair, and there was, in her whole attitude, an expression of despair and prostration; one would have said that she no longer believed in the resurrection of her beloved Lord. In truth, the Christ was that day of such a sallow, greenish hue that it was difficult to imagine that life could ever return to His decomposing flesh. All the other people in the picture seemed to share that feeling; their eyes were dull, their expressions mournful, and their halos gave forth only a leaden gleam; the livid hue of death had invaded that canvas formerly so warm and full of life.

Tiburce was deeply touched by the expression of supreme melancholy upon the Magdalen's face, and his resolution to depart was shaken. He preferred to attribute it to a secret sympathy rather than to a caprice of the light. The weather was dull, the rain cut the sky with slender threads, and a ray of daylight, drenched with water and mist, forced its way with difficulty through the glass, streaming and beaten by the wing of the squall; that reason was much too plausible to be admitted by Tiburce.

"Ah!" he said to himself in an undertone, quoting a verse of one of our young poets, "'How I would love thee tomorrow if thou wert living!' – Why art thou only an impalpable ghost attached forever to the meshes of this canvas and held captive by this thin layer of varnish? Why art thou the phantom of life, without the power to live? What does it profit thee to be lovely, noble, and great, to have in thine eyes the flame of earthly love and of divine love, and about thy head the resplendent halo of repentance, being simply a little oil and paint spread on canvas in a certain way? Oh! lovely adored one, turn toward me for an instant that glance, at once so soft and so dazzling; sinner, take pity upon an insane passion, thou, to whom love opened the gates of Heaven; descend from that frame, stand erect in thy long, green satin skirt; for it is a long while that thou hast knelt before the sublime scaffold; these holy women will guard the body without thee and will suffice for the death vigil. Come, Magdalen, come! thou hast not emptied all thy jars of perfume at the feet of the Divine Master! there must remain enough of nard and cinnamon in the bottom of thy onyx jar to renew the luster of thy hair, dimmed by the ashes of repentance. Thou shalt have, as of yore, strings of pearls, Negro pages, and coverlets of the purple of Sidon. Come, Magdalen, although thou hast been two thousand years dead, I have enough of youth and ardor to reanimate thy dust. Ah! specter of beauty, let me but hold thee in my arms one instant, then let me die!"

A stifled sigh, as faint and soft as the wail of a dove mortally wounded, echoed sadly in the air. Tiburce thought that the Magdalen had answered him.

It was Gretchen, who, hidden behind a pillar, had seen all, heard all, understood all. Something had broken in her heart; she was not loved.

That evening Tiburce came to see her; he was pale and depressed. Gretchen was as white as wax. The excitement of the morning had driven the color from her cheeks, like the powder from the wings of a butterfly.

"I start for Paris tomorrow; will you come with me?"

"To Paris or elsewhere; wherever you please," replied Gretchen, in whom every shred of will-power seemed extinct; "shall I not be unhappy everywhere?"

Tiburce flashed a keen and searching glance at her.

"Come tomorrow morning; I will be ready; I have given you my heart and my life. Dispose of your servant."

She went with Tiburce to the Arms of Brabant, to assist him to make his preparations for departure; she packed his books, his linen, and his pictures, then she returned to her little room on Rue Kipdorp; she did not undress, but threw herself fully dressed upon her bed.

An unconquerable depression had seized upon her soul; everything about her seemed sad: the bouquets were withered in their blue glass vases; the lamps flickered and cast a dim and intermittent light; the ivory Christ bent His head in despair upon His breast; and the blessed boxwood assumed the aspect of a cypress dipped in lustral water.

The little Virgin from her little recess watched her in surprise with her enamel eyes; and the storm, pressing his knee against the window-pane, made the lead partitions groan and creak.

The heaviest furniture, the most unimportant utensils, wore an expression of intelligence and compassion; they cracked dolorously and gave forth mournful sounds. The easy chair held out its long, unoccupied arms; the hop-vine on the trellis passed its little green hand familiarly through a broken pane; the kettle complained and wept among the ashes; the curtains of the bed fell in more lifeless and more distressed folds; the whole room seemed to understand that it was about to lose its young mistress. Gretchen called her old servant, who wept bitterly; she handed her her keys and the certificates of her little income, then opened the cage of her two-coffee-colored turtle-doves and set them free.

The next morning she was on her way to Paris with Tiburce.

VI
FROM THE CANVAS

Tiburce's apartment greatly surprised the young Antwerp maiden, accustomed to Flemish strictness and method. That mixture of luxury and heedlessness upset all her ideas. For instance, a crimson velvet cover was thrown upon a wretched broken table; magnificent candelabra of the most ornate style, which would not have been out of place in the boudoir of a king's mistress, were supplied with paltry bodices of common glass, which the candles, burning down to the very bottom, had burst; a china vase of beautiful material and workmanship and of great value had received a kick in the side, and its splintered fragments were held together by iron wire; exceedingly rare engravings were fastened to the wall by pins; a Greek cap was on the head of an antique Venus, and a multitude of incongruous objects, such as Turkish pipes, narghiles, daggers, yataghans, Chinese shoes, and Indian slippers, encumbered the chairs and whatnots.

The painstaking Gretchen had no rest until all this was cleaned, neatly hung, and labeled; like God who made the world from chaos, she made of that medley a delightful apartment. Tiburce, who was accustomed to its confusion and who knew perfectly where things ought not to be, had difficulty at first in recognizing his surroundings; but he ended by becoming used to it. The objects which he disarranged returned to their places as if by magic. He realized for the first time what comfort meant. Like all imaginative people, he neglected details. The door of his bedroom was gilded and covered with arabesques, but it had no weather-strips; like the genuine savage that he was, he loved splendor and not well-being; he would have worn, like the Orientals, waistcoats of gold brocade lined with toweling.

And yet, although he seemed to enjoy this more human and more reasonable mode of life, he was often sad and distraught; he would remain whole days upon his divan, flanked by two piles of cushions, with eyes closed and hands hanging, and not utter a word; Gretchen dared not question him, she was so afraid of his reply. The scene in the cathedral had remained engraved upon her memory, in painful and ineffaceable strokes.

He continued to think of the Magdalen at Antwerp; absence made her more beautiful in his sight; he saw her before him like a luminous apparition. An imaginary sunlight riddled her hair with rays of gold, her dress had the transparency of an emerald, her shoulders gleamed like Parian marble. Her tears had dried, and youth shone in all its bloom upon, the down of her rosy cheeks; she seemed entirely consoled for the death of the Christ; whose bluish white foot she supported heedlessly, while she turned her face towards her earthly lover. The rigid outlines of sanctity were softened and had become undulating and supple; the sinner reappeared in the person of the penitent; her neckerchief floated more freely, her skirt swelled out in alluring and worldly folds, her arms were amorously outstretched, as if ready to seize a victim of love. The great saint had become a courtesan, and had transformed herself into a temptress. In a more credulous age Tiburce would have seen therein some underhand machination of him who goes prowling about, "seeking whom he may devour"; he would have believed that the devil's claw was upon his shoulder and that he was bewitched in due form.

How did it happen that Tiburce, beloved by a charming young girl, simple of heart, and endowed with intelligence, possessed of beauty, youth, innocence, all the real gifts which come from God, and which no one can acquire, persisted in pursuing a mad chimera, an impossible dream; and how could that mind, so keen and powerful, have arrived at such a degree of aberration? Such things are seen every day; have we not, each one of us in our respective spheres, been loved obscurely by some humble heart, while we sought more exalted loves? Have not we trodden under foot a pale violet with its timid perfume, while striding along with lowered eyes toward a cold and gleaming star which cast its ironic glance upon us from the depths of infinity? Has not the abyss its magnetism and the impossible its fascination?

One day Tiburce entered Gretchen's chamber carrying a bundle; he took from it a skirt and waist of green satin, made after the antique style, a chemisette of a shape long out of fashion, and a string of huge pearls. He requested Gretchen to put on those garments, which could not fail to be most becoming to her, and to keep them in the house; he told her by way of explanation that he was very fond of. sixteenth-century costumes, and that by falling in with that fancy of his she would confer very great pleasure upon him. You will readily believe that a young girl did not need to be asked twice to try on a new gown; she was soon dressed, and when she entered the salon, Tiburce could not withhold a cry of surprise and admiration. He found something to criticize, however, in the headdress, and, releasing the hair from the teeth of the comb, he spread it out in great curls over Gretchen's shoulders, like the Magdalen's hair in the Descent from the Cross. That done, he gave a different twist to some folds of the skirt, loosened the laces of the waist, rumpled the neckerchief, which was too stiff and starchy, and, stepping back a few feet, contemplated his work.

Doubtless you have seen what are called living pictures, at some special performance. The most beautiful actresses are selected, and dressed and posed in such wise as to reproduce some familiar painting. Tiburce had achieved a masterpiece of that sort; you would have said that it was a bit cut from Ruben's canvas.

Gretchen made a movement.

"Don't stir, you will spoil the pose; you are so lovely thus!" cried Tiburce in a tone of entreaty.

The poor girl obeyed and remained motionless for several minutes. When she turned, Tiburce saw that her face was bathed in tears.

He realized that she knew all.

Gretchen's tears flowed silently down her cheeks, without contraction of the features, without effort, like pearls overflowing from the too full cup of her eyes, lovely azure flowers of divine limpidity; grief could not mar the harmony of her face, and her tears were lovelier than another woman's smile.

Gretchen wiped them away with the back of her hand, and leaning upon the arm of a chair, she said in a voice tremulous and melting with emotion:

"Oh, how you have made me suffer, Tiburce! Jealousy of a new sort wrung my heart; although I had no rival, I was betrayed nonetheless; you loved a painted woman; she possessed your thoughts, your dreams; she alone seemed fair to you, who saw only her in all the world; plunged in that mad contemplation, you did not even see that I had wept. And I believed for an instant that you loved me, whereas I was simply a duplicate, a counterfeit of your passion! I know well that in your eyes I am only an ignorant little girl who speaks French with a German accent that makes you laugh; my face pleases you as a reminder of your imaginary mistress; you see in me a pretty manikin which you drape according to your fancy; but I tell you the manikin suffers and loves you."

Tiburce tried to draw her to his heart, but she released herself and continued:

"You talked to me enchantingly of love, you taught me that I was lovely and charming to look upon, you pressed my hands and declared that no fairy had smaller ones; you said of my hair that it was more precious than a prince's golden cloak, and of my eyes that the angels came down from Heaven to look at themselves in them, and that they stayed so long that they were late in returning and were scolded by the good Lord; and all this in a sweet and penetrating voice, with an accent of truth that would have deceived those more experienced than I. Alas! my resemblance to the Magdalen in the picture kindled your imagination and gave you that artificial eloquence; she answered you through my mouth; I gave her the life that she lacks, and I served to complete your illusion. If I have given you a few moments of happiness, I forgive you for making me play this part. After all, it is not your fault if you do not know how to love, if the impossible alone attracts you, if you long only for that which you cannot attain. You are ambitious to love, you are deceived concerning yourself, you will never love. You must have perfection, the ideal and poesy – all those things which do not exist.' Instead of loving in a woman the love that she has for you, of being grateful to her for her devotion and for the gift of her heart, you look to see if she resembles that plaster Venus in your study. Woe to her if the outline of her brow has not the desired curve! You are concerned about the grain of her skin, the shade of her hair, the fineness of her wrists and her ankles, but never about her heart. You are not a lover, poor Tiburce, you are simply a painter. What you have taken for passion is simply admiration for shape and beauty; you were in love with the talent of Rubens, not with the Magdalen; your vocation of painter stirred vaguely within you and produced those frantic outbursts which you could not control. Thence came all the degradation of your fantasy. I have discovered this, because I love you. Love is a woman's genius, her mind is not engrossed in selfish contemplation! Since I have been here I have turned over your books, I have read your poets, I have become almost a scholar. The veil has fallen from my eyes. I have discovered many things that I should never have suspected. Thus I have been able to read clearly in your heart. You used to draw – take up your pencils again. You must place your dreams upon canvas, and all this great agitation will calm down of itself. If I cannot be your mistress, I will at all events be your model."

She rang and told the servant to bring an easel, canvas, colors, and brushes.

When the servant had prepared everything, the chaste girl suddenly let her garments fall to the floor with sublime immodesty, and raising her hair, like Aphrodite come forth from the sea, stood in the bright light.

"Am I not as lovely as your Venus of Milo?" she asked with a sweet little pout.

After two hours, the face was already alive and half protruding from the canvas; in a week it was finished. It was not a perfect picture, however; but an exquisite touch of refinement and of purity, a wonderful softness of tone, and the noble simplicity of the arrangement made it noteworthy, especially to connoisseurs. That slender white and fair-haired figure, standing forth in an unconstrained attitude against the twofold azure of the sky and the sea, and presenting herself to the world nude and smiling, had a reflection of antique poesy and recalled the best periods of Greek sculpture.

Tiburce had already forgotten the Magdalen of Antwerp.

"Well!" said Gretchen, "are you satisfied with your model?"

"When would you like to publish our banns?" was Tiburce's reply.

"I shall be the wife of a great painter," she said, throwing her arms about her lover's neck; "but do not forget, monsieur, that it was I who discovered your genius, that priceless jewel – I, little Gretchen of Rue Kipdorp!"

La Morte Amoureuse

I
A STRANGE STORY

Brother, you ask me if I have ever loved. Yes. My story is a strange and terrible one; and though I am sixty-six years of age, I scarcely dare even now to disturb the ashes of that memory. To you I can refuse nothing; but I should not relate such a tale to any less experienced mind. So strange were the circumstances of my story, that I can scarcely believe myself to have ever actually been a party to them. For more than three years I remained the victim of a most singular and diabolical illusion. Poor country priest though I was, I led every night in a dream – would to God it had been all a dream! – a most worldly life, a damning life, a life of a Sardanapalus. One single look too freely cast upon a woman well-nigh caused me to lose my soul; but finally by the grace of God and the assistance of my patron saint, I succeeded in casting out the evil spirit that possessed me. My daily life was long interwoven with a nocturnal life of a totally different character. By day I was a priest of the Lord, occupied with prayer and sacred things; by night, from the instant that I closed my eyes I became a young nobleman, a fine connoisseur in women, dogs, and horses; gambling, drinking, and blaspheming; and when I awoke at early daybreak, it seemed to me, on the other hand, that I had been sleeping, and had only dreamed that I was a priest. Of this somnambulistic life there now remains to me only the recollection of certain scenes and words which I cannot banish from my memory; but although I never actually left the walls of my presbytery, one would think to hear me speak that I were a man who, weary of all worldly pleasures, had become a religious, seeking to end a tempestuous life in the service of God, rather than an humble seminarist who has grown old in this obscure curacy, situated in the depths of the woods and even isolated from the life of the century.

Yes, I have loved as none in the world ever loved – with an insensate and furious passion – so violent that I am astonished it did not cause my heart to burst asunder. Ah, what nights – what nights!

From my earliest childhood I had felt a vocation to the priesthood, so that all my studies were directed with that idea in view. Up to the age of twenty-four my life had been only a prolonged novitiate. Having completed my course of theology, I successively received all the minor orders, and my superiors judged me worthy, despite my youth, to pass the last awful degree. My ordination was fixed for Easter week.

I had never gone into the world. My world was confined by the walls of the college and the seminary. I knew in a vague sort of a way that there was something called Woman, but I never permitted my thoughts to dwell on such a subject, and I lived in a state of perfect innocence. Twice a year only I saw my infirm and aged mother, and in those visits were comprised my sole relations with the outer world.

I regretted nothing; I felt not the least hesitation at taking the last irrevocable step; I was filled with joy and impatience. Never did a betrothed lover count the slow hours with more feverish ardor; I slept only to dream that I was saying mass; I believed there could be nothing in the world more delightful than to be a priest; I would have refused to be a king or a poet in preference. My ambition could conceive of no loftier aim.

I tell you this in order to show you that what happened to me could not have happened in the natural order of things, and to enable you to understand that I was the victim of an inexplicable fascination.

At last the great day came. I walked to the church with a step so light that I fancied myself sustained in air, or that I had wings upon my shoulders. I believed myself an angel, and wondered at the somber and thoughtful faces of my companions, for there were several of us. I had passed all the night in prayer, and was in a condition well-nigh bordering on ecstasy. The bishop, a venerable old man, seemed to me God the Father leaning over his Eternity, and I beheld Heaven through the vault of the temple.

You well know the details of that ceremony – the benediction, the communion under both forms, the anointing of the palms of the hands with the Oil of Catechumens, and then the holy sacrifice offered in concert with the bishop.

Ah, truly spake Job when he declared that the imprudent man is one who hath not made a covenant with his eyes! I accidentally lifted my head, which until then I had kept down, and beheld before me, so close that it seemed that I could have touched her – although she was actually a considerable distance from me and on the further side of the sanctuary railing – a young woman of extraordinary beauty, and attired with royal magnificence. It seemed as though scales had suddenly fallen from my eyes. I felt like a blind man who unexpectedly recovers his sight. The bishop, so radiantly glorious but an instant before, suddenly vanished away, the tapers paled upon their golden candlesticks like stars in the dawn, and a vast darkness seemed to fill the whole church. The charming creature appeared in bright relief against the background of that darkness, like some angelic revelation. She seemed herself radiant, and radiating light rather than receiving it.

I lowered my eyelids, firmly resolved not to again open them, that I might not be influenced by external objects, for distraction had gradually taken possession of me until I hardly knew what I was doing.

In another minute, nevertheless, I reopened my eyes, for through my eyelashes I still beheld her, all sparkling with prismatic colors, and surrounded with such a purple penumbra as one beholds in gazing at the sun.

Oh, how beautiful she was! The greatest painters, who followed ideal beauty into heaven itself, and thence brought back to earth the true portrait of the Madonna, never in their delineations even approached that wildly beautiful reality which I saw before me. Neither the verses of the poet nor the palette of the artist could convey any conception of her. She was rather tall, with a form and bearing of a goddess. Her hair, of a soft blonde hue, was parted in the midst and flowed back over her temples in two rivers of rippling gold; she seemed a diademed queen. Her forehead, bluish-white in its transparency, extended its calm breadth above the arches of her eyebrows, which by a strange singularity were almost black, and admirably relieved the effect of sea-green eyes of unsustainable vivacity and brilliancy. What eyes! With a single flash they could have decided a man's destiny. They had a life, a limpidity, an ardor, a humid light which I have never seen in human eyes; they shot forth rays like arrows, which I could distinctly see enter my heart. I know not if the fire which illumined them came from heaven or from hell, but assuredly it came from one or the other. That woman was either an angel or a demon, perhaps both. Assuredly she never sprang from the flank of Eve, our common mother. Teeth of the most lustrous pearl gleamed in her ruddy smile, and at every inflection of her lips little dimples appeared in the satiny rose of her adorable cheeks. There was a delicacy and pride in the regal outline of her nostrils bespeaking noble blood. Agate gleams played over the smooth lustrous skin of her half-bare shoulders, and strings of great blonde pearls – almost equal to her neck in beauty of color – descended upon her bosom. From time to time she elevated her head with the undulating grace of a startled serpent or peacock, thereby imparting a quivering motion to – the high lace ruff which surrounded it like a silver trelliswork.

She wore a robe of orange-red velvet, and from her wide ermine-lined sleeves there peeped forth patrician hands of infinite delicacy, and so ideally transparent that, like the fingers of Aurora, they permitted the light to shine through them.

All these details I can recollect at this moment as plainly as though they were of yesterday, for notwithstanding I was greatly troubled at the time, nothing escaped me; the faintest touch of shading, the little dark speck at the point of the chin, the imperceptible down at the corners of the lips, the velvety floss upon the brow, the quivering shadows of the eyelashes upon the cheeks – I could notice everything with astonishing lucidity of perception.

And gazing, I felt opening within me gates that had until then remained closed; vents long obstructed became all clear, permitting glimpses of unfamiliar perspectives within; life suddenly made itself visible to me under a totally novel aspect. I felt as though I had just been born into a new world and a new order of things. A frightful anguish commenced to torture my heart as with red-hot pincers. Every successive minute seemed to me at once but a second and yet a century. Meanwhile the ceremony was proceeding, and I shortly found myself transported far from that world of which my newly born desires were furiously besieging the entrance. Nevertheless I answered "Yes" when I wished to say "No," though all within me protested against the violence done to my soul by my tongue. Some occult power seemed to force the words from my throat against my will. Thus it is, perhaps, that so many young girls walk to the altar firmly resolved to refuse in a startling manner the husband imposed upon them, and that yet not one ever fulfils her intention. Thus it is, doubtless, that so many poor novices take the veil, though they have resolved to tear it into shreds at the moment when called upon to utter the vows. One dares not thus cause so great a scandal to all present, nor deceive the expectation of so many people. All those eyes, all those wills seem to weigh down upon you like a cope of lead; and, moreover, measures have been so well taken, everything has been so thoroughly arranged beforehand and after a fashion so evidently irrevocable, that the will yields to the weight of circumstances and utterly breaks down.

As the ceremony proceeded the features of the fair unknown changed their expression. Her look had at first been one of caressing tenderness; it changed to an air of disdain and of mortification, as though at not having been able to make itself understood.

With an effort of will sufficient to have uprooted a mountain, I strove to cry out that I would not be a priest, but I could not speak; my tongue seemed nailed to my palate, and I found it impossible to express my will by the least syllable of negation. Though fully awake, I felt like one under the influence of a nightmare, who vainly strives to shriek out the one word upon which life depends.

She seemed conscious of the martyrdom I was undergoing, and, as though to encourage me, she gave me a look replete with divinest promise. Her eyes were a poem; their every glance was a song.

She said to me:

"If thou wilt be mine, I shall make thee happier than God Himself in His paradise. The angels themselves will be jealous of thee. Tear off that funeral shroud in which thou art about to wrap thyself. I am Beauty, I am Youth, I am Life. Come to me! Together we shall be Love. Can Jehovah offer thee aught in exchange? Our lives will flow on like a dream, in one eternal kiss.

"Fling forth the wine of that chalice, and thou art free. I will conduct thee to the Unknown Isles. Thou shalt sleep in my bosom upon a bed of massy gold under a silver pavilion, for I love thee and would take thee away from thy God, before whom so many noble hearts pour forth floods of love which never reach even the steps of His throne!"

These words seemed to float to my ears in a rhythm of infinite sweetness, for her look was actually sonorous, and the utterances of her eyes were reechoed in the depths of my heart as though living lips had breathed them into my life. I felt myself willing to renounce God, and yet my tongue mechanically fulfilled all the formalities of the ceremony. The fair one gave me another look, so beseeching, so despairing the keen blades seemed to pierce my heart, and I felt my bosom transfixed by more swords than those of Our Lady of Sorrows.

II
ROOT IMPERISHABLE

All was consummated: I had become a priest.

Never was deeper anguish painted on human face than upon hers. The maiden who beholds her affianced lover suddenly fall dead at her side, the mother bending over the empty cradle of her child, Eve seated at the threshold of the gate of Paradise, the miser who finds a stone substituted for his stolen treasure, the poet who accidentally permits the only manuscript of his finest work to fall into the fire, could not wear a look so despairing, so inconsolable. All the blood had abandoned her charming face, leaving it whiter than marble; her beautiful arms hung lifelessly on either side of her body as though their muscles had suddenly relaxed, and she sought the support of a pillar, for her yielding limbs almost betrayed her. As for myself, I staggered toward the door of the church, livid as death, my forehead bathed with a sweat bloodier than that of Calvary; I felt as though I were being strangled; the vault seemed to have flattened down upon my shoulders, and it seemed to me that my head alone sustained the whole weight of the dome.

As I was about to cross the thresh-hold a hand suddenly caught mine – a woman's hand! I had never till then touched the hand of any woman. It was cold as a serpent's skin, and yet its impress remained upon my wrist, burned there as though branded by a glowing iron. It was she. "Unhappy man! Unhappy man! What hast thou done?" she exclaimed in a low voice, and immediately disappeared in the crowd.

The aged bishop passed by. He cast a severe and scrutinizing look upon me. My face presented the wildest aspect imaginable; I blushed and turned pale alternately; dazzling lights flashed before my eyes. A companion took pity on me. He seized my arm and led me out. I could not possibly have found my way back to the seminary unassisted. At the corner of a street, while the young priest's attention was momentarily turned in another direction, a Negro page, fantastically garbed, approached me, and without pausing on his way slipped into my hand a little pocketbook with gold-embroidered corners, at the same time giving me a sign to hide it. I concealed it in my sleeve, and there kept it until I found myself alone in my cell. Then I opened the clasp. There were only two leaves within, bearing the words, "Clarimonde. At the Concini Palace." So little acquainted was I at that time with the things of this world that I had never heard of Clarimonde, celebrated as she was, and I had no idea as to where die Concini Palace was situated. I hazarded a thousand conjectures, each more extravagant than the last; but, in truth, I cared little whether she were a great lady or a courtesan, so that I could but see her once more.

My love, although the growth of a single hour, had taken imperishable root. I did not even dream of attempting to tear it up, so fully was I convinced such a thing would be impossible. That woman had completely taken possession of me. One look from her had sufficed to change my very nature. She had breathed her will into my life, and I no longer lived in myself, but in her and for her. I gave myself up to a thousand extravagancies. I kissed the place upon my hand which she had touched, and I repeated her name over and over again for hours in succession. I only needed to close my eyes in order to see her distinctly as though she were actually present; and I reiterated to myself the words she had uttered in my ear at the church porch: "Unhappy man! Unhappy man! What hast thou done?" I comprehended at last the full horror of my situation, and the funereal and awful restraints of the state into which I had just entered became clearly revealed to me. To be a priest! – that is, to be chaste, to never love, to observe no distinction of sex or age, to turn from the sight of all beauty, to put out one's own eyes, to hide forever crouching in the chill shadows of some church or cloister, to visit none but the dying, to watch by unknown corpses, and ever bear about with one the black soutane as a garb of mourning for one's self, so that your very dress might serve as a pall for your coffin.

And I felt life rising within me like a subterranean lake, expanding and overflowing; my blood leaped fiercely through my arteries; my long-restrained youth suddenly burst into active being, like the aloe which blooms but once in a hundred years, and then bursts into blossom with a clap of thunder.

What could I do in order to see Clarimonde once more? I had no pretext to offer for desiring to leave the seminary, not knowing any person in the city. I would not even be able to remain there but a short time, and was only waiting my assignment to the curacy which I must thereafter occupy. I tried to remove the bars of the window; but it was at a fearful height from the ground, and I found that as I had no ladder it would be useless to think of escaping thus. And, furthermore, I could descend thence only by night in any event, and afterward how should I be able to find my way through the inextricable labyrinth of streets? All these difficulties, which to many would have appeared altogether insignificant, were gigantic to me, a poor seminarist who had fallen in love only the day before for the first time, with-out experience, without money, without attire.

"Ah!" cried I to myself in my blindness, "were I not a priest I could have seen her every day; I might have been her lover, her spouse. Instead of being wrapped in this dismal shroud of mine I would have had garments of silk and velvet, golden chains, a sword, and fair plumes like other handsome young cavaliers. My hair, instead of being dishonored by the tonsure, would flow down upon my neck in waving curls; I would have a fine waxed mustache; I would be a gallant." But one hour passed before an altar, a few hastily articulated words, had forever cut me off from the number of the living, and I had myself sealed down the stone of my own tomb; I had with my own hand bolted the gate of my prison!

I went to the window. The sky was beautifully blue; the trees had donned their spring robes; nature seemed to be making parade of an ironical joy. The Place was filled with people, some going, others coming; young beaux and young beauties were sauntering in couples toward the groves and gardens; merry youths passed by, cheerily trolling refrains of drinking songs – it was all a picture of vivacity, life, animation, gayety, which formed a bitter contrast with my mourning and my solitude. On the steps of the gate sat a young mother playing with her child. She kissed its little rosy mouth still impearled with drops of milk, and performed, in order to amuse it, a thousand divine little puerilities such as only mothers know how to invent. The father standing at a little distance smiled gently upon the charming group, and with folded arms seemed to hug his joy to his heart. I could not endure that spectacle. I closed the window with violence, and flung myself on my bed, my heart filled with frightful hate and jealousy, and gnawed my fingers and my bedcovers like a tiger that has passed ten days without food.

I know not how long I remained in this condition, but at last, while writhing on the bed in a fit of spasmodic fury, I suddenly perceived the Abbé Serapion, who was standing erect in the center of the room, watching me attentively. Filled with shame of myself, I let my head fall upon my breast and covered my face with my hands.

"Romuald, my friend, something very extraordinary is transpiring within you," observed Serapion, after a few moments' silence; "your conduct is altogether inexplicable. You – always so quiet, so pious, so gentle – you to rage in your cell like a wild beast! Take heed, brother – do not listen to the suggestions of the devil. The Evil Spirit, furious that you have consecrated yourself forever to the Lord, is prowling around you like a ravening wolf and making a last effort to obtain possession of you. Instead of allowing yourself to be conquered, my dear Romuald, make to yourself a cuirass of prayers, a buckler of mortifications, and combat the enemy like a valiant man; you will then assuredly overcome him. Virtue must be proved by temptation, and gold comes forth purer from the hands of the assayer. Fear not. Never allow yourself to become discouraged. The most watchful and steadfast souls are at moments liable to such temptation. Pray, fast, meditate, and the Evil Spirit will depart from you."

The words of the Abbé Serapion re-stored me to myself, and I became a little more calm. "I came," he continued, ".to tell you that you have been appointed to the curacy of C——. The priest who had charge of it has just died, and Monseigneur the Bishop has ordered me to have you installed there at once. Be ready, therefore, to start tomorrow." I responded with an inclination of the head, and the Abbé retired. I opened my missal and commenced reading some prayers, but the letters became confused and blurred under my eyes, the thread of the ideas entangled itself hopelessly in my brain, and the volume at last fell from my hands without my being aware of it.

To leave tomorrow without having been able to see her again, to add yet another barrier to the many already interposed between us, to lose forever all hope of being able to meet her, except, indeed, through a miracle! Even to write her, alas! would be impossible, for by whom could I dispatch my letter? With my sacred character of priest, to whom could I dare unbosom myself, in whom could I confide? I became a prey to the bitterest anxiety.

Then suddenly recurred to me the words of the Abbé Serapion regarding the artifices of the devil; and the strange character of the adventure, the supernatural beauty of Clarimonde, the phosphoric light of her eyes, the burning imprint of her hand, the agony into which she had thrown me, the sudden change wrought within me when all my piety vanished in a single instant – these and other things clearly testified to the work of the Evil One, and perhaps that satiny hand was but the glove which concealed his claws. Filled with terror at these fancies, I again picked up the missal which had slipped from my knees and fallen upon the floor, and once more gave myself up to prayer.

III
SEA-GREEN EYES

Next morning Serapion came to take me away. Two mules freighted with our miserable valises awaited us at the gate. He mounted one, and I the other as well as I knew how.

As we passed along the streets of the city, I gazed attentively at all the windows and balconies in the hope of seeing Clarimonde, but it was yet early in the morning, and the city had hardly opened its eyes. Mine sought to penetrate the blinds and window-curtains of all the palaces before which we were passing. Serapion doubtless attributed this curiosity to my admiration of the architecture, for he slackened the pace of his animal in order to give me time to look around me. At last we passed the city gates and commenced to mount the hill beyond. When we arrived at its summit I turned to take a last look at the place where Clarimonde dwelt. The shadow of a great cloud hung, over all the city;

the contrasting colors of its blue and red roofs were lost in the uniform half-tint, through which here and there floated upward, like white flakes of foam, the smoke of freshly kindled fires. By a singular optical effect one edifice, which surpassed in height all the neighboring buildings that were still dimly veiled by the vapors, towered up, fair and lustrous with the gilding of a solitary beam of sunlight – although actually more than a league away it seemed quite near. The smallest details of its architecture were plainly distinguishable – the turrets, the platforms, the window-casements, and even the swallow-tailed weather-vanes.

"What is that palace I see over there, all lighted up by the sun?" I asked Serapion. He shaded his eyes with his hand, and having looked in the direction indicated, replied: "It is the ancient palace which the Prince Concini has given to the courtesan Clarimonde. Awful things are done there!"

At that instant, I know not yet whether it was a reality or an illusion, I fancied I saw gliding along the terrace a shapely white figure, which gleamed for a moment in passing and as quickly vanished. It was Clarimonde.

Oh, did she know that at that very hour, all feverish and restless – from the height of the rugged road which separated me from her and which, alas! I could never more descend – I was directing my eyes upon the palace where she dwelt, and which a mocking beam of sunlight seemed to bring nigh to me, as though inviting me to enter therein as its lord? Undoubtedly she must have known it, for her soul was too sympathetically united with mine not to have felt its least emotional thrill, and that subtle sympathy it must have been which prompted her to climb – although clad only in her night-dress – to the summit of the terrace, amid the icy dews of the morning.

The shadow gained the palace, and the scene became to the eye only a motionless ocean of roofs and gables, amid which one mountainous undulation was distinctly visible. Serapion urged his mule forward, my own at once followed at the same – gait, and a sharp angle in the road at last hid the city of S—— forever from my eyes, as I was destined never to return thither. At the close of a weary three-days' journey through dismal country fields, we caught sight of the cock upon the steeple of the church which I was to take charge of, peeping above the trees, and after having followed some winding roads fringed with thatched cottages and little gardens, we found ourselves in front of the façade, which certainly possessed few features of magnificence. A porch ornamented with some moldings, and two or three pillars rudely hewn from sandstone; a tiled roof with counterforts of the same sandstone as the pillars – that was all. To the left lay the cemetery overgrown with high weeds, and having a great iron cross rising up in its center; to the right stood the presbytery, under the shadow of the church. It was a house of the most extreme simplicity and frigid cleanliness. We entered the enclosure. A few chickens were picking up some oats scattered upon the ground; accustomed, seemingly, to the black habit of ecclesiastics, they showed no fear of our presence and scarcely troubled themselves to get out of our way. A hoarse, wheezy barking fell upon our ears, and we saw an aged dog running toward us.

It was my predecessor's dog. He had dull bleared eyes, grizzled hair, and every mark of the greatest age to which a dog can possibly attain. I patted him gently, and he proceeded at once to march along beside me with an air of satisfaction unspeakable. A very old woman, who had been the housekeeper of the former curé, also came to meet us, and after having invited me into a little back parlor, asked whether I intended to retain her. I replied that I would take care of her, and the dog, and the chickens, and all the furniture her master had bequeathed her at his death. At this she became fairly transported with joy, and the Abbé Serapion at once paid her the price which she asked for her little property.

As soon as my installation was over, the Abbé Serapion returned to the seminary. I was, therefore, left alone, with no one but myself to look to for aid or counsel. The thought of Clarimonde again began to haunt me, and in spite of all my endeavors to banish it, I always found it present in my meditations. One evening while promenading in my little garden along the walks bordered with box-plants, I fancied that I saw through the elm trees the figure of a woman, who followed my every movement, and that I beheld two sea-green eyes gleaming through the foliage; but it was only an illusion, and on going round to the other side of the garden, I could find nothing except a footprint on the sanded walk – a footprint so small that it seemed to have been made by the foot of a child. The garden was enclosed by very high walls. I searched every nook and corner of it, but could discover no one there. I have never succeeded in fully accounting for this circumstance, which, after all, was nothing compared with the strange things which happened to me afterward.

For a whole year I lived thus, filling all the duties of my calling with the most scrupulous exactitude, praying and fasting, exhorting and lending ghostly aid to the sick, and bestowing alms even to the extent of frequently depriving myself of the very necessaries of life.

But I felt a great aridness within me, and the sources of grace seemed closed against me. I never found that happiness which should spring from the fulfillment of a holy mission: my thoughts were far away, and the words of Clarimonde were ever upon my lips like an involuntary refrain. Oh, brother, meditate well on this! Through having but once lifted my eyes to look upon a woman, through one fault apparently so venial, I have for years remained a victim to the most miserable agonies, and the happiness of my life has been destroyed forever.

I will not longer dwell upon those defeats, or on those inward victories invariably followed by yet more terrible falls, but will at once proceed to the facts of my story. One night my doorbell was long and violently rung. The aged housekeeper arose and opened to the stranger, and the figure of a man, whose complexion was deeply bronzed, and who was richly clad in a foreign costume, with a poniard at his girdle, appeared under the rays of Barbara's lantern. Her first impulse was one of terror, but the stranger reassured her, and stated that he desired to see me at once on matters relating to my holy calling. Barbara invited him upstairs, where I was on the point of retiring. The stranger told me that his mistress, a very noble lady, was lying at the point of death, and desired to see a priest. I replied that I was prepared to follow him, took with me the sacred articles necessary for extreme unction, and descended in all haste. Two horses black as the night itself stood without the gate, pawing the ground with impatience, and veiling their chests with long streams of smoky vapor exhaled from their nostrils. He held the stirrup and aided me to mount upon one; then, merely laying his hand upon the pummel of the saddle, he vaulted on the other, pressed the animal's sides with Ms knees, and loosened rein. The horse bounded forward with the velocity of an arrow. Mine, of which the stranger held the bridle, also started off at a swift gallop, keeping up with his companion. We devoured the road. The ground flowed backward beneath us in a long streaked line of pale grey, and the black silhouettes of the trees seemed fleeing by us on either side like an army in rout. We passed through a forest so profoundly gloomy that I felt my flesh creep in the chill darkness with superstitious fear. The showers of bright sparks which flew from the stony road under the irons both feet of our horses remained glowing in our wake like a fiery trail; and had anyone at that hour of the night beheld us both – my guide and myself – he must have taken us for two specters riding upon nightmares. Witch-fires ever and anon flitted across the road before us, and the night-birds shrieked fearsomely in the depth of the woods beyond, where we beheld at intervals glow the phosphorescent eyes of wildcats. The manes of the horses became more and more disheveled, the sweat streamed over their flanks, and their breath came through their nostrils hard and fast. But when he found them slacking pace, the guide reanimated them by uttering a strange, guttural, unearthly cry, and the gallop recommenced with fury. At last the whirlwind race ceased; a huge black mass pierced through with many bright points of light suddenly rose before us, the hoofs of our horses echoed louder upon a great vaulted archway which darkly yawned between two enormous towers. Some great excitement evidently reigned in the castle. Servants with torches were crossing the courtyard in every direction, and above, lights were ascending and descending from landing to landing. I obtained a confused glimpse of vast masses of architecture – columns, arcades, flights of steps, stairways – a royal voluptuousness and elfin magnificence of construction worthy of fairyland. A Negro page – the same who had before brought me the tablet from Clarimonde, and whom I instantly recognized – approached to aid me in dismounting, and the major-domo, attired in black velvet with a gold chain about his neck, advanced to meet me, supporting himself upon an ivory cane. Large tears were falling from his eyes and streaming over his cheeks and white beard. "Too late!" he cried, sorrowfully shaking his venerable head. "Too late, sir priest! But if you have not been able to save the soul, come at least and watch by the poor body."

He took my arm and conducted me to the death chamber. I wept not less bitterly than he, for I had learned that the dead one was none other than that Clarimonde whom I had so deeply and so wildly loved. A prie-dieu stood at the foot of the bed; a bluish flame flickering in a bonze patera filled all the room with a wan, deceptive light, here and there bringing out in the darkness at intervals some projection of furniture or cornice. In a chiseled urn upon the table there was a faded white rose, whose leaves – excepting one that still held – had all fallen, like odorous tears, to the foot of the vase. A broken black mask, a fan, and disguises of every variety, which were lying on the armchairs, bore witness that death had entered suddenly and unannounced into that sumptuous dwelling. Without daring to cast my eyes upon the bed, I knelt down and commenced to repeat the Psalms for the Dead, with exceeding fervor, thanking God that he had placed the tomb between me and the memory of this woman, so that I might thereafter be able to utter her name in my prayers as a name forever sanctified by death. But my fervor gradually weakened, and I fell insensibly into a reverie. That chamber bore no semblance to a chamber of death. In lieu of the fetid and cadaverous odors which I had been accustomed to breathe during such funereal vigils, a languorous vapor of Oriental perfume – I know not what amorous odor of woman – softly floated through the tepid air. That pale light seemed rather a twilight gloom contrived for voluptuous pleasure than a substitute for the yellow-flickering watch tapers which shine by the side of corpses. I thought upon the strange destiny which enabled me to meet Clarimonde again at the very moment when she was lost to me forever, and a sigh of regretful anguish escaped from my breast. Then it seemed to me that someone behind me had also sighed, and I turned round to look. It was only an echo. But in that moment my eyes fell upon the bed of death which they had till then avoided. The red damask curtains, decorated with large flowers worked in embroidery, and looped up with gold bullion, permitted me to behold the fair dead, lying at full length, with hands joined upon her bosom. She was covered with a linen wrapping of dazzling whiteness, which formed a strong contrast with the gloomy purple of the hangings, and was of so fine a texture that it concealed nothing of her body's charming form, and allowed the eye to follow those beautiful outlines – undulating like the neck of a swan – which even death had not robbed of their supple grace. She seemed an alabaster statue executed by some skillful sculptor to place upon the tomb of a queen, or rather, perhaps, like a slumbering maiden over whom the silent snow had woven a spotless veil.

I could no longer maintain my constrained attitude of prayer. The air of the alcove intoxicated me, that febrile perfume of half-faded roses penetrated my very brain, and I commenced to pace restlessly up and down the chamber, pausing at each turn before the bier to contemplate the graceful corpse lying beneath the transparency of its shroud. Wild fancies came thronging to my brain. I thought to myself that she might not, perhaps, be really dead; that she might only have feigned death for the purpose of bringing me to her castle, and then declaring her love. At one time I even thought I saw her foot move under the whiteness of the coverings, and slightly disarrange the long, straight folds of the winding-sheet.

And then I asked myself: "Is this indeed Clarimonde? What proof have I that it is she? Might not that black page have passed into the service of some other lady? Surely, I must be going mad to torture and afflict myself thus!" But my heart answered with a fierce throbbing: "It is she; it is she indeed!" I approached the bed again, and fixed my eyes with redoubled attention upon the object of my incertitude. Ah, must I confess it? That exquisite perfection of bodily form, although purified and made sacred by the shadow of death, affected me more voluptuously than it should have done, and that repose so closely resembled slumber that one might well have mistaken it for such. I forgot that I had come there to perform a funeral ceremony; I fancied myself a young bridegroom entering the chamber of the bride, who all modestly hides her fair face, and through coyness seeks to keep herself wholly veiled. Heartbroken with grief, yet wild with hope, shuddering at once with fear and pleasure, I bent over her and grasped the corner of the sheet. I lifted it back, holding my breath all the while through fear of waking her. My arteries throbbed with such violence that I felt them hiss through my temples, and the sweat poured from my forehead in streams, as though I had lifted a mighty slab of marble. There, indeed, lay Clarimonde, even as I had seen her at the church on the day of my ordination. She was not less charming than then. With her, death seemed but a last coquetry. The pallor of her cheeks, the less brilliant carnation of her lips, her long eyelashes lowered and relieving their dark fringe against that white skin, lent her an unspeakably seductive aspect of melancholy chastity and metal suffering; her long loose hair, still intertwined with some little blue flowers, made a shining pillow for her head, and veiled the nudity of her shoulders with its thick ringlets; her beautiful hands, purer, more diaphanous than the Host, were crossed on her bosom in an attitude of pious rest and silent prayer, which served to counteract all that might have proven otherwise too alluring – even after death – in the exquisite roundness and ivory polish of her bare arms from which the pearl bracelets had not yet been removed. I remained long in mute contemplation, and the more I gazed, the less could I persuade myself that life had really abandoned that beautiful body forever. I do not know whether it was an illusion or a reflection of the lamplight, but it seemed to me that the blood was again commencing to circulate under that lifeless pallor, although she remained all motionless. I laid my hand lightly on her arm; it was cold, but not colder than her hand on the day when it touched mine at the portals of the church. I resumed my position, bending my face above her, and bathing her cheeks with the warm dew of my tears. Ah, what bitter feelings of despair and helplessness, what agonies unutterable did I endure in that long watch! Vainly did I wish that I could have gathered all my life into one mass that I might give it all to her, and breathe into her chill remains the flame which devoured me. The night advanced, and feeling the moment of eternal separation approach, I could not deny myself the last sad sweet pleasure of imprinting a kiss upon the dead lips of her who had been my only love. . . Oh, miracle! A faint breath mingled itself with my breath, and the mouth of Clarimonde responded to the passionate pressure of mine. Her eyes unclosed, and lighted up with something of their former brilliancy; she uttered a long sigh, and uncrossing her arms, passed them around my neck with a look of ineffable delight. "Ah, it is thou, Romuald!" she murmured in a voice languishingly sweet as the last vibrations of a harp. "What ailed thee, dearest? I waited so long for thee that I am dead; but we are now betrothed; I can see thee and visit thee. Adieu, Romuald, adieu! I love thee. That is all I wished to tell thee, and I give thee back the life which thy kiss for a moment recalled. We shall soon meet again."

Her head fell back, but her arms yet encircled me, as though to retain me still. A furious whirlwind suddenly burst in the window, and entered the chamber. The last remaining leaf of the white rose for a moment palpitated at the extremity of the stalk like a butterfly's wing, then it detached itself and flew forth through the open casement, bearing with it the soul of Clarimonde. The lamp was extinguished, and I fell insensible upon the bosom of the beautiful dead.

IV
A VICTIM

When I came to myself again I was lying on the bed in my little room at tie presbytery, and the old dog of the former curé was licking my hand which had been hanging down outside of the covers. Barbara, all trembling with age and anxiety, was busying herself about the room, opening and shutting drawers, and emptying powders into glasses. On seeing me open my eyes, the old woman uttered a cry of joy, the dog yelped and wagged his tail, but I was still so weak that I could not speak a single word or make the slightest motion. Afterward I learned that I had lain thus for three days, giving no evidence of life beyond the faintest respiration. Those three days do not reckon in my life, nor could I ever imagine whither my spirit had departed during those three days; I have no recollection of aught relating to them. Barbara told me that the same coppery-complexioned man who came to seek me on the night of my departure from the presbytery, had brought me back the next morning in a close litter, and departed immediately afterward. When I became able to collect my scattered thoughts, I reviewed within my mind all the circumstances of that fateful night. At first I thought I had been the victim of some magical illusion, but ere long the recollection of other circumstances, real and palpable in themselves, came to forbid that supposition. I could not believe that I had been dreaming, since Barbara as well as myself had seen the strange man with his two black horses, and described with exactness every detail of his figure and apparel. Nevertheless it appeared that none knew of any castle in the neighborhood answering to the description of that in which I had again found Clarimonde.

One morning I found the Abbé Serapion in my room. Barbara had advised him that I was ill, and he had come with all speed to see me. Although this haste on his part testified to an affectionate interest in me, yet his visit did not cause me the pleasure which it should have done. The Abbé Serapion had something penetrating and inquisitorial in his gaze which made me feel very ill at ease. His presence filled me with embarrassment and a sense of guilt. At the first glance he divined my interior trouble, and I hated him for his clairvoyance. While he inquired after my health in hypocritically honeyed accents, he constantly kept his two great yellow lion-eyes fixed upon me, and plunged his look into my soul like a sounding lead. Then he asked me how I directed my parish, if I was happy in it, how I passed the leisure hours allowed me in the intervals of pastoral duty, whether I had become acquainted with many of the inhabitants of the place, what was my favorite reading, and a thousand other such questions. I answered these inquiries as briefly as possible, and he, without ever waiting for my answers, passed rapidly from one subject of query to another. That conversation had evidently no connection with what he actually wished to say. At last, without any premonition, but as though repeating a piece of news which he had recalled on the instant, and feared might otherwise be forgotten subsequently, he suddenly said, in a clear vibrant voice, which rang in my ears like the trumpets of the Last Judgment:

"The great courtesan Clarimonde died a few days ago, at the close of an orgy which lasted eight days and eight nights. It was something infernally splendid. The abominations of the banquets of Belshazzar and Cleopatra were reenacted there. Good God, what age are we living in? The guests were served by swarthy slaves who spoke an unknown tongue, and who seemed to me to be veritable demons. The livery of the very least among them would have served for the gala-dress of an emperor. There have always been very strange stories told of this Clarimonde, and all her lovers came to a violent or miserable end. They used to say that she was a ghoul, a female vampire; but I believe she was none other than Beelzebub himself."

He ceased to speak and commenced to regard me more attentively than ever, as though to observe the effect of his words on me. I could not refrain from starting when I heard him utter the name of Clarimonde, and this news of her death, in addition to the pain it caused me by reason of its coincidence with the nocturnal scenes I had witnessed, filled me with an agony and terror which my face betrayed, despite my utmost – endeavors to appear composed. Serapion fixed an anxious and severe look upon me, and then observed: "My son, I must warn you that you are standing with foot raised upon the brink of an abyss; take heed lest you fall therein. Satan's claws are long, and tombs are not always true to their trust. The tombstone of Clarimonde should be sealed down with a triple seal, for, if report be true, it is not the first time she has died. May God watch over you, Romuald!"

And with these words the Abbé walked slowly to the door. I did not see him again at that time, for he left for S—— almost immediately.

I became completely restored to health and resumed my accustomed duties. The memory of Clarimonde and the words of the old Abbé were constantly in my mind; nevertheless no extraordinary event had occurred to verify the funereal predictions of Serapion, and I had commenced to believe that his fears and my own terrors were overexaggerated, when one night I had a strange dream. I had hardly fallen asleep when I heard my bed-curtains drawn apart, as their rings slided back upon the curtain rod with a sharp sound. I rose up quickly upon my elbow, and beheld the shadow of a woman standing erect before me. I recognized Clarimonde immediately. She bore in her hand a little lamp, shaped like those which are placed in tombs, and its light lent her fingers a rosy transparency, which extended itself by lessening degrees even to the opaque and milky whiteness of her bare arm. Her only garment was the linen winding-sheet which had shrouded her when lying upon the bed of death. She sought to gather its folds over her bosom as though ashamed of being so scantily clad, but her little hand was not equal to the task. She was so white that the color of the drapery blended with that of her flesh under the pallid rays of the lamp. Enveloped with this subtle tissue which betrayed all the contours of her body, she seemed rather the marble statue of some fair antique bather than a woman endowed with life. But dead or living, statue or woman, shadow or body, her beauty was still the same, only that the green light of her eyes was less brilliant, and her mouth, once so warmly crimson, was only tinted with a faint tender rosy-ness, like that of her cheeks. The little blue flowers which I had noticed entwined in her hair were withered and dry, and had lost nearly all their leaves, but this did not prevent her from being charming – so charming that notwithstanding the strange character of the adventure, and the unexplainable manner in which she had entered my room, I felt not even for a moment the least fear.

She placed the lamp on the table and seated herself at the foot of my bed; then bending toward me, she said, in that voice at once silvery clear and yet velvety in its sweet softness, such as I never heard from any lips save hers:

"I have kept thee long in waiting, dear Romuald, and it must have seemed to thee that I had forgotten thee. But I come from afar off, very far off, and from a land whence no other has ever yet returned. There is neither sun nor moon in that land whence I come: all is but space and shadow; there is neither road nor pathway: no earth for the foot, no air for the wing; and nevertheless behold me here, for Love is stronger than Death and must conquer him in the end. Oh what sad faces and fearful things I have seen on my way hither! What difficulty my soul, returned to earth through the power of will alone, has had in finding its body and reinstating itself therein! What terrible efforts I had to make ere I could lift the ponderous slab with which they had covered me! See, the palms of my poor hands are all bruised! Kiss them, sweet love, that they may be healed!" She laid the cold palms of her hands upon my mouth, one after the other. I kissed them, indeed, many times, and she the while watched me with a smile of ineffable affection.

I confess to my shame that I had entirely forgotten the advice of the Abbé Serapion and the sacred office wherewith I had been invested. I had fallen without resistance, and at the first assault. I had not even made the least effort to repel the tempter. The fresh coolness of Clarimonde skin penetrated my own, and I felt voluptuous tremors pass over my whole body. Poor child! in spite of all I saw afterward, I can hardly yet believe she was a demon; at least she had no appearance of being such, and never did Satan so skillfully conceal his claws and horns. She had drawn her feet up beneath her, and squatted down on the edge of the couch in an attitude full of negligent coquetry. From time to time she passed her little hand through my hair and twisted it into curls, as though trying how a new style of wearing it would become my face. I abandoned myself to her hands with the most guilty pleasure, while she accompanied her gentle play with the prettiest prattle. The most remarkable fact was that I felt no astonishment whatever at so extraordinary an adventure, and as in dreams one finds no difficulty in accepting the most fantastic events as simple facts, so all these circumstances seemed to me perfectly natural in themselves.

"I loved thee long ere I saw thee, dear Romuald, and sought thee everywhere. Thou wast my dream, and I first saw thee in the church at the fatal moment. I said at once, 'It is he!' I gave thee a look into which I threw all the love I ever had, all the love I now have, all the love I shall ever have for thee – a look that would have damned a cardinal or brought a king to his knees at my feet in view of all his court. Thou remainedst unmoved, preferring thy God to me!

"Ah, how jealous I am of that God whom thou didst love and still lovest more than me!

"Woe is me, unhappy one that I am! I can never have thy heart all to myself, I whom thou didst recall to life with a kiss – dead Clarimonde, who for thy sake bursts asunder the gates of the tomb, and comes to consecrate to thee a life which she has resumed only to make thee happy!"

All her words were accompanied with the most impassioned caresses, which bewildered my sense and my reason to such an extent, that I did not fear to utter a frightful blasphemy for the sake of consoling her, and to declare that I loved her as much as God.

Her eyes rekindled and shone like chrysoprases. "In truth? – in very truth? – as much as God!" she cried, flinging her beautiful arms around me. "Since it is so, thou wilt come with me; thou wilt follow me whithersoever I desire. Thou wilt cast away thy ugly black habit. Thou shalt be the proudest and most envied of cavaliers; thou shalt be my lover! To be the acknowledged lover of Clarimonde, who has refused even a Pope; that will be something to feel proud of! Ah, the fair, unspeakably happy existence, the beautiful golden life we shall live together! And when shall we depart, my fair sir?"

"Tomorrow! Tomorrow!" I cried in my delirium.

"Tomorrow, then, so let it be!" she answered. "In the meanwhile I shall have opportunity to change my toilet, for this is a little too light and in nowise suited for a voyage. I must also forthwith notify all my friends who believe me dead, and mourn for me as deeply as they are capable of doing The money, the dresses, the carriages-all will be ready. I shall call for thee at this same hour. Adieu, dear heart!" And she lightly touched my forehead with her lips. The lamp went out, the curtains closed again, and all became dark; a leaden, dreamless sleep fell on me and held me unconscious until the morning following.

V
SERAPION'S MATTOCK

I awoke later than usual, and the recollection of this singular adventure troubled me during the whole day. I finally persuaded myself that it was a mere vapor of my heated imagination. Nevertheless its sensations had been so vivid that it was difficult to persuade myself that they were not real, and it was not without some presentiment of what was going to happen that I got into bed at last, after having prayed God to drive far from me all thoughts of evil, and to protect the chastity of my slumber.

I soon fell into a deep sleep, and my dream was continued. The curtains again parted, and I beheld Clarimonde, not as on the former occasion, pale in her pale winding-sheet, with the violets of death upon her cheeks, but gay, sprightly, jaunty, in a superb traveling dress of green velvet, trimmed with gold lace, and looped up on either side to allow a glimpse of satin petticoat. Her blonde hair escaped in thick ringlets from beneath a broad black felt hat, decorated with white feathers whimsically twisted into various shapes. In one hand she held a little riding whip terminated by a golden whistle. She tapped me lightly with it, and exclaimed: "Well, my fine sleeper, is this the way you make your preparations? I thought I would find you up and dressed. Arise quickly, we have no time to lose."

I leaped out of bed at once.

"Come, dress yourself, and let us go," she continued, pointing to a little package she had brought with her. "The horses are becoming impatient of delay and champing their bits at the door. We ought to have been by this time at least ten leagues distant from here."

I dressed myself hurriedly, and she handed me the articles of apparel herself one by one, bursting into laughter from time to time at my awkwardness, as she explained to me the use of a garment when I had made a mistake. She hurriedly arranged my hair, and this done, held up before me a little pocket mirror of Venetian crystal, rimmed with silver filigree-work, and playfully asked: "How dost find thyself now? Wilt engage me for thy valet de chambre?"

I was no longer the same person, and I could not even recognize myself. I resembled my former self no more than a finished statue resembles a block of stone. My old face seemed but a coarse daub of the one reflected in the mirror. I was handsome, and my vanity was sensibly tickled by the metamorphosis. That elegant apparel, that richly embroidered vest had made of me a totally different personage, and I marveled at the power of transformation owned by a few yards of cloth cut after a certain pattern. The spirit of my costume penetrated my very skin, and within ten minutes more I had become something of a coxcomb.

In order to feel more at ease in my new attire, I took several turns up and down the room. Clarimonde watched me with an air of maternal pleasure, and appeared well satisfied with her work. "Come, enough of this child's-play! Let us start, Romuald, dear. We have far to go, and we may not get there in time." She took my hand and led me forth. All the doors opened before her at a touch, and we passed by the dog without awaking him.

At the gate we found Margheritone waiting, the same swarthy groom who had once before been my escort. He held the bridles of three horses, all black like those which bore us to the castle – one for me, one for him, one for Clarimonde. Those horses must have been Spanish genets born of mares fecundated by a zephyr, for they were fleet as the wind itself, and the moon, which had just risen at our departure to light us on the way, rolled over the sky like a wheel detached from her own chariot. We beheld her on the right leaping from tree to tree, and putting herself out of breath in the effort to keep up with us. Soon we came upon a level plain where, hard by a clump of trees, a carriage with four vigorous horses awaited us. We entered it, and the postilions urged their animals into a mad gallop. I had one arm around Clarimonde's waist, and one of her hands clasped in mine; her head leaned upon my shoulder, and I felt her bosom, half bare, lightly pressing against my arm. I had never known such intense happiness. In that hour I had forgotten everything, and I no more remembered having ever been a priest than I remembered what I had been doing in my mother's womb, so great was the fascination which the evil spirit exerted upon me. From that night my nature seemed in some sort to have become halved, and there were two men within me, neither of whom knew the other. At one moment I believed my-self a priest who dreamed nightly that he was a gentleman, at another that I was a gentleman who dreamed he was a priest. I could no longer distinguish the dream from the reality, nor could I discover where the reality began or where ended the dream. The exquisite young lord and libertine railed at the priest, the priest loathed the dissolute habits of the young lord. Two spirals entangled and confounded the one with the other, yet never touching, would afford a fair representation of this bucolic life which I lived. Despite the strange character of my condition, I do not believe that I ever inclined, even for a moment, to madness. I always retained with extreme vividness all the perceptions of my two lives. Only there was one absurd fact which I could not explain to myself – namely, that the consciousness of the same individuality existed in two men so opposite in character. It was an anomaly for which I could not account – whether I believed myself to be the curé of the little village of C——, or II Signor Romualdo, the titled lover of Clarimonde. Be that as it may, I lived, at least I believed that I lived, in Venice. I have never been able to discover rightly how much of illusion and how much of reality there was in this fantastic adventure. We dwelt in a great palace on the Canaleio, filled with frescoes and statues, and containing two Titians in the noblest style of the great master, which were hung in Clarimonde's chamber. It was a palace well worthy of a king. We had each our gondola, our barcarolli in family livery, our music hall, and our special poet. Clarimonde always lived upon a magnificent scale; there was something of Cleopatra in her nature. As for me, I had the retinue of a prince's son, and I was regarded with as much reverential respect as though I had been of the family of one of the twelve Apostles or the four Evangelists of the Most Serene Republic. I would not have turned aside to allow even the Doge to pass, and I do not believe that since Satan fell from heaven, any creature was ever prouder or more insolent than I. I went to the Ridotto, and played with a luck which seemed absolutely infernal. I received the best of all society – the sons of ruined families, women of the theater, shrewd knaves, parasites, hectoring swashbucklers. But notwithstanding the dissipation of such a life, I always remained faithful to Clarimonde. I loved her wildly. She would have excited satiety itself, and chained inconstancy. To have Clarimonde was to have twenty mistresses; aye, to possess all women; so mobile, so varied of aspect, so fresh in new charms was she all in herself – a very chameleon of a woman, in sooth. She made you commit with her the infidelity you would have committed with another, by donning to perfection the character, the attraction, the style of beauty of the woman who appeared to please you. She returned my love a hundred-fold, and it was in vain that the young patricians and even the Ancients of the Council of Ten made her the most magnificent proposals. A Foscari even went so far as to offer to espouse her. She rejected all his overtures. Of gold she had enough. She wished no longer for anything but love – a love youthful, pure, evoked by herself, and which should be a first and last passion. I would have been perfectly happy but for a cursed nightmare which recurred every night, and in which I believed myself to be a poor village curé, practicing mortification and penance for my excesses during the day. Reassured by my constant association with her, I never thought further of the strange manner in which I had become acquainted with Clarimonde. But the words of the Abbé Serapion concerning her recurred often to my memory, and never ceased to cause me uneasiness.

For some time the health of Clarimonde had not been so good as usual; her complexion grew paler day by day. The physicians who were summoned could not comprehend the nature of her malady and knew not how to treat it. They all prescribed some insignificant remedies, and never called a second time. Her paleness, nevertheless, visibly increased, and she became colder and colder, until she seemed almost as white and dead as upon that memorable night in the unknown castle. I grieved with anguish unspeakable to behold her thus slowly perishing; and she, touched by my agony, smiled upon me sweetly and sadly with the fateful smile of those who feel that they must die.

One morning I was seated at her bedside, and breakfasting from a little table placed close at hand, so that I might not be obliged to leave her for a single instant. In the act of cutting some fruit I accidentally inflicted rather a deep gash on my finger. The blood immediately gushed forth in a little purple jet, and a few drops spurted upon Clarimonde. Her eyes flashed, her face suddenly assumed an expression of savage and ferocious joy such as I had never before observed in her. She leaped out of her bed with animal agility – the agility, as it were, of an ape or a cat – and sprang upon my wound, which she commenced to suck with an air of unutterable pleasure. She swallowed the blood in little mouthfuls, slowly and carefully, like a connoisseur tasting a wine from Xeres or Syracuse. Gradually her eyelids half closed, and the pupils of her green eyes became oblong instead of round. From time to time she paused in order to kiss my hand, then she would recommence to press her lips to the lips of the wound in order to coax forth a few more ruddy drops. When she found that the blood would no longer come, she arose with eyes liquid and brilliant, rosier than a May dawn; her face full and fresh, her hand warm and moist – in fine, more beautiful than ever, and in the most perfect health.

"I shall not die! I shall not die!" she cried, clinging to my neck, half mad with joy. "I can love thee yet for a long time. My life is thine, and all that is of me comes from thee. A few drops of thy rich and noble blood, more precious and more potent than all the elixirs of the earth, have given me back life."

This scene long haunted my memory, and inspired me with strange doubts in regard to Clarimonde; and the same evening, when slumber had transported me to my presbytery, I beheld the Abbé Serapion, graver and more anxious of aspect than ever. He gazed attentively at me, and sorrowfully exclaimed: "Not content with losing your soul, you now desire also to lose your body. Wretched young man, into how terrible a plight have you fallen'!" The tone in which he uttered these words powerfully affected me, but in spite of its vividness even that impression was soon dissipated, and a thousand other cares erased it from my mind. At last one evening, while looking into a mirror whose traitorous position she had not taken into account, I saw Clarimonde in the act of emptying a powder into the cup of spiced wine which she had long been in the habit of preparing after our repasts. I took the cup, feigned to carry it to my lips, and then placed it on the nearest article of furniture as though intending to finish it at my leisure. Taking advantage of a moment when the fair one's back was turned, I threw the contents under the table, after which I retired to my chamber and went to bed, fully resolved not to sleep, but to watch and discover what should come of all this mystery. I did not have to wait long. Clarimonde entered in her night-dress, and having removed her apparel, crept into bed and lay down beside me. When she felt assured that I was asleep, she bared my arm, and drawing a gold pin from her hair, commenced to murmur in a low voice:

"One drop, only one drop! One ruby at the end of my needle! Since thou lovest me yet, I must not die! . . . Ah, poor love! His beautiful blood, so brightly purple, I must drink it. Sleep, my only treasure! Sleep, my god, my child! I will do thee no harm; I will only take of thy life what I must to keep my own from being forever extinguished. But that I love thee so much, I could well resolve to have other lovers whose veins I could drain; but since I have known thee all other men have become hateful to me. . . . Ah, the beautiful arm! How round it is! How white it is! How shall I ever dare to prick this pretty blue vein!" And while thus murmuring to herself she wept, and I felt her tears raining on my arm as she clasped it with her hands. At last she took the resolve, slightly punctured me with her pin, and commenced to suck up the blood which oozed from the place. Although she swallowed only a few drops, the fear of weakening me soon seized her, and she carefully tied a little band around my arm, afterward rubbing the wound with an unguent which immediately cicatrized it.

Further doubts were impossible. The Abbé Serapion was right. Notwithstanding this positive knowledge, however, I could not cease to love Clarimonde, and I would gladly of my own accord have, given her all the blood she required to sustain her factitious life. Moreover, I felt but little fear of her. The woman seemed – to plead with me for the vampire, and what I had already heard and seen sufficed to reassure me completely. In those days I had plenteous veins, which would not have been so easily exhausted as at present; and I would not have thought of bargaining for my blood, drop by drop. I would rather have opened myself the veins of my arm and said to her: "Drink, and may my love infiltrate itself throughout thy body together with my blood!" I carefully avoided ever making the least reference to the narcotic drink she had prepared for me, or to the incident of the pin, and we lived in the most perfect harmony.

Yet my priestly scruples commenced to torment me more than ever, and I was at a loss to imagine what new penance I could invent in order to mortify and subdue my flesh. Although these visions were involuntary, and though I did not actually participate in anything relating to them, I could not dare to touch the body of Christ with hands so impure and a mind defiled by such debauches whether real or imaginary. In the effort to avoid falling under the influence of these wearisome hallucinations, I strove to prevent myself from being overcome by sleep. I held my eyelids open with my fingers, and stood for hours together leaning upright against the wall, fighting sleep with all my might; but the dust of drowsiness invariably gathered upon my eyes at last, and finding all resistance useless, I would have to let my arms fall in the extremity of despairing weariness, and the current of slumber would again bear me away to the perfidious shores. Serapion addressed me with the most vehement exhortations, severely reproaching me for my softness and want of fervor. Finally, one day when I was more wretched than usual, he said to me: "There is but one way by which you can obtain relief from this continual torment, and though it is an extreme measure it must be made use of; violent diseases require violent remedies. I know where Clarimonde is buried. It is necessary that we shall disinter her remains, and that you shall behold in how pitiable a state the object of your love is. Then you will no longer be tempted to lose your soul for the sake of an unclean corpse devoured by worms, and ready to crumble into dust. That will assuredly restore you to yourself." For my part, I was so tired of this double life that I at once consented, desiring to ascertain beyond a doubt whether a priest or a gentleman had been the victim of delusion. I had become fully resolved either to kill one of the two men within me for the benefit of the other, or else to kill both, for so terrible an existence could not last long and be endured. The Abbé Serapion provided himself with a mattock, a lever, and a lantern, and at midnight we wended our way to the cemetery of ——, the location and place of which were perfectly familiar to him. After having directed the rays of the dark lantern upon the inscriptions of several tombs, we came at last upon a great slab, half concealed by huge weeds and devoured by mosses and parasitic plants, whereupon we deciphered the opening lines of the epitaph:

HERE LIES CLARIMONDE
WHO WAS FAMED IN HER LIFE-TIME
AS THE FAIREST OF WOMEN.

"It is here without a doubt," muttered Serapion, and placing his lantern on the ground, he forced the point of the lever under the edge of the stone and commenced to raise it. The stone yielded, and he proceeded to work with the mattock. Darker and more silent than the night itself, I stood by and watched him do it, while he, bending over his dismal toil, streamed with sweat, panted, and his hard-coming breath seemed to have the harsh tone of a death rattle. It was a weird scene, and had any persons from without beheld us, they would assuredly have taken us rather for profane wretches and shroud-stealers than for priests of God. There was something grim and fierce in Serapion's zeal which lent him the air of a demon rather than of an apostle or an angel, and his great aquiline face, with all its stern features brought out in strong relief by the lantern-light, had something fearsome in it which enhanced the unpleasant fancy. I felt an icy sweat come out upon my forehead in huge beads, and my hair stood up with a hideous fear. Within the depths of my own heart I felt that the act of the austere Serapion was an abominable sacrilege; and I could have prayed that a triangle of fire would issue from the entrails of the dark clouds, heavily rolling above us, to reduce him to cinders. The owls which had been nestling in the cypress trees, startled by the gleam of the lantern, flew against it from time to time, striking their dusty wings against its panes, and uttering plaintive cries of lamentation; wild foxes yelped in the far darkness, and a thousand sinister noises detached themselves from the silence. At last Serapion's mattock struck the coffin itself, making its planks reecho with a deep sonorous sound, with that terrible sound nothingness utters when stricken. He wrenched apart and tore up the lid, and I beheld Clarimonde, pallid as a figure of marble, with hands joined; her white winding-sheet made but one fold from her head to her feet. A little crimson drop sparkled like a speck of dew at one corner of her colorless mouth. Serapion, at this spectacle, burst into fury: "Ah, thou art here, demon! Impure courtesan! Drinker of blood and gold!" And he flung holy water upon the corpse and the coffin, over which he traced the sign of the cross withies sprinkler. Poor Clarimonde had no sooner been touched by the blessed spray than her beautiful body crumbled into dust, and became only a shapeless and frightful mass of cinders and half-calcined bones.

"Behold your mistress, my Lord Romuald!" cried the inexorable priest, as he pointed to these sad remains. "Will you be easily tempted after this to promenade on the Lido or at Fusina with your beauty?" I covered my face with my hands, a vast ruin had taken place within me. I returned to my presbytery, and the noble Lord Romuald, the lover of Clarimonde, separated himself from the poor priest with whom he had kept such strange company so long. But once only, the following night, I saw Clarimonde. She said to me, as she had said the first time at the portals of the church: "Unhappy man! Unhappy man! What hast thou done? Wherefore have hearkened to that imbecile priest? Wert thou not happy? And what harm had I ever done thee that thou shouldst violate my poor tomb, and lay bare the miseries of my nothingness? All communication between our souls and our bodies is henceforth forever broken. Adieu! Thou wilt yet regret me!" She vanished in air as smoke, and I never saw her more.

Alas! she spoke truly indeed. I have regretted her more than once, and I regret her still. My soul's peace has been very dearly bought. The love of God was not too much to replace such a love as hers. And this, brother, is the story of my youth. Never gaze upon a woman, and walk abroad only with eyes ever fixed upon the ground; for however chaste and watchful one may be, the error of a single moment is enough to make one lose eternity.

THE END

www.ingramcontent.com/pod-product-compliance
Lightning Source LLC
Chambersburg PA
CBHW030418310726
48979CB00007B/1106